BEACON STREET GIRLS

This book belongs to:

VERITAS AMICITIA GAUDIUM
truth friendship fun!

Be sure to read all of our books:

BSG Special Adventure Books:

Coming Soon:

BEACON STREET GIRLS

Katani's Jamaican Holiday

BY
ANNIE BRYANT

ALADDIN MIX

NEW YORK   LONDON   TORONTO   SYDNEY

ALADDIN MIX

Simon & Schuster Children's Publishing Division

1230 Avenue of the Americas, New York, NY 10020

Copyright © 2008 by B*tween Productions, Inc.,

Home of the Beacon Street Girls

Beacon Street Girls, Kgirl, B*tween Productions, B*Street, and the characters Maeve, Avery, Charlotte, Isabel, Katani, Marty, Nick, Anna, Joline, and Happy Lucky Thingy are registered trademarks and/or copyrights of B*tween Productions, Inc.

All rights reserved, including the right of reproduction in whole or in part in any form.

ALADDIN PAPERBACKS, ALADDIN MIX, and related logo are registered trademarks of Simon & Schuster, Inc.

Designed by Dina Barsky

The text of this book was set in Palatino Linotype.

Manufactured in the United States of America

First Aladdin Paperbacks edition June 2008

2 4 6 8 10 9 7 5 3 1

Library of Congress Control Number 2008920653

ISBN-13: 978-1-4169-6443-8

ISBN-10: 1-4169-6443-6

Who's Who

BSG

Katani Summers
a.k.a. Kgirl ... Katani has a strong fashion sense and business savvy. She is stylish, loyal & cool.

Avery Madden
Avery is passionate about all sports and animal rights. She is energetic, optimistic & outspoken.

Charlotte Ramsey
A self-acknowledged "klutz" and an aspiring writer, Charlotte is all too familiar with being the new kid in town. She is intelligent, worldly & curious.

Isabel Martinez
Her ambition is to be an artist. She was the last to join the Beacon Street Girls. She is artistic, sensitive & kind.

Maeve Kaplan-Taylor
Maeve wants to be a movie star. Bubbly and upbeat, she wears her heart on her sleeve. She is entertaining, friendly & fun.

Ms. Razzberry Pink
The stylishly pink proprietor of the "Think Pink" boutique is chic, gracious & charming.

Marty
The adopted best dog friend of the Beacon Street Girls is feisty, cuddly & suave.

Happy Lucky Thingy and **alter ego Mad Nasty Thingy**
Marty's favorite chew toy, it is known to reveal its alter ego when shaken too roughly. He is most often happy.

more on beaconstreetgirls.com

We'd like to thank our friends at the Jamaica Tourist Board who arranged for us to visit Jamaica! We'd like to thank all the resorts, attractions, and tour operators who spent so much time showing us around and telling us about Jamaica. A huge thank-you to the schools we visited while we were there and a big, warm, Beacon Street Girl hug to the students who gave us such wonderful ideas for the adventures in this book. Many thanks to our talented friend Sean Kingston. A special thank-you to Hazel Campbell, who contributed much of the content and Jamaican warmth and friendliness found within these pages.

We'd also like to send a big shout-out to:

Air Jamaica
Airports Authority of Jamaica
The Institute of Jamaica
The National Gallery of Jamaica
Fae
Carol
Troy
Marcia
Yvonne, and of course, Ariella

1

An Important Letter

My dear Ruby,

I know it has been a long time since I have written. I do hope you and the family are well. In your letters to me over the years you have always expressed a desire to visit Jamaica, the home of your mother's birth, and I would so love to see you before the days run out.

My bakery is doing well. Though it is small, it keeps body and soul together. I bake a very tasty banana bread—nice and moist and flavorful. Truth is I can't produce enough to fill the demand. Everybody loves Nana's Banana Bliss.

Well, for some time I have been putting off some surgery, but can't do so any longer. On the 15th I will be going into the hospital. Now don't worry. It's just something I need to take care of. But I will have to close the bakery because the young girl who's there just can't manage on her own. The rest of the family can't really help out. I couldn't bring in a stranger.

But I really don't want to close it and lose my customers or my growing momentum.

Another bakery has been trying to cut me out of the business. You see, there's a man, Mr. Biggs, who owns this bakery, and he has offered to buy me out. He only wants to use my famous name, Nana's Banana Bliss, to sell his cheaper, not better, banana bread. I've made it known that I am not selling to that man, so he has been trying every which way to steal my customers and force me out of business. What do you think of someone who would do such a thing to an old woman like me? If I close the bakery, even for a week, I'm afraid it will give him just the opportunity he needs to destroy our business.

I know you are a busy person. We are so proud of you, Principal Ruby, but my dear, we need your help desperately. Do you think you could get some time off, even just a week, while I have surgery, to come and supervise the bakery for me? I would be really very grateful, and as I said, it would be very nice to finally meet you. And if you like, please bring one of your granddaughters along. Jamaica is such a beautiful place to visit, and it is the home of your ancestors.

> *I am,*
> *Your loving aunt*
> *Faith*

Grandma Ruby finished reading, took off her glasses, and set them down on our kitchen table with a little sigh. When she looked up at me she had a faraway look in her eyes. I glanced at the letter with the Jamaican stamp she was holding and wondered if anything was wrong. But before I could say anything, Grandma cocked her head to one side and asked, "Katani, how would you like to go with me to Jamaica?"

Hello! Visions of beautiful beaches, palm trees, and pineapple drinks with little umbrellas began swirling through my brain.

CHAPTER
2

A Jamaican Welcome

W ow, Grandma. This airport is crazy cool." I directed my grandma's attention to a small band with two guitarists and a drummer playing some kind of box instrument. I remembered from the Jamaican guidebook I flipped through before we left that it was called a "mento band." A group of women shook their rattles as they sang a "Welcome to Jamaica" song to a lively reggae beat. I was definitely not in Boston anymore.

The Jamaican ladies were dressed in white blouses trimmed with the same colorful plaid material of their skirts. The yellow and green colors of Jamaica adorned their heads, and they wore funky-looking rope sandals. The men in the band coordinated with the women. I decided to call their look "Island Chill."

"We sure are on vacation!" Grandma Ruby laughed as I pulled out my Kgirl Island Inspiration Notebook and starting scribbling my first impressions of Jamaican style.

Kgirl's Island Inspiration Notebook

A designer's notes on REAL Jamaican style!

1. "Island Chill": Tuscan gold (my favorite color!) and ivy green plaid—is it a national costume? LOVE the headwraps!

At home I usually carry around a notebook so I can jot down business and style ideas 24/7, because my goal is to have my own Kgirl fashion design company one day. So for this trip I bought a special, brand-new notebook with a yellow-black-green-striped cover (the colors of the Jamaican flag!) to record all the colors, patterns, textures, and even smells, tastes, and feelings of Jamaica. I read in a magazine that really original designers are inspired by everything around them, and it's totally true. I grabbed my camera and started taking pictures, too. I didn't want to forget anything about my trip.

Some of the people who were on the plane with us began dancing and greeting the singers. It was embarrassing. I couldn't believe the American travelers in their weird Bermuda shorts were thinking they were reggae dancers. I quickly hid behind Grandma Ruby, who, for some reason I couldn't understand, was clapping along with the dancing tourists.

"Grandma, whatever you do, please don't dance," I whispered. She just laughed and began to sway with the music. Then I thought of my good friend Maeve. She would have started hip-hopping away with the dancers and everybody would have loved her ability to dance up a storm. She would have fit right in. I wasn't even going to try—not today, anyway.

"Baggage call for Air Jamaica flight 211 on carousel three." Saved by the bell! I grabbed Grandma's arm and headed for the carousel. We had only one suitcase each, and our luggage came pretty quickly, which was great because I wanted to get outside and find myself a beautiful Jamaican beach!

After the redcap wheeled us out, our next task was to find Selvin, Aunt Faith's nephew, who was supposed to meet us. Grandma had no idea what he looked like, so I figured we would be at the airport for a while. I just hoped there would be a beach near my relatives' house. I couldn't wait to get out the shades, the sunscreen, and sandals. Jamaican holiday, here I come!

Outside Sangster International Airport, chaos reigned. Tourists were everywhere, climbing into tour buses and taxis that would take them to their various hotels. There were friendly cabbies inviting us in, asking which hotel we were staying at, and trying to be helpful. After some minutes with no sign of Selvin, this option was looking really good.

Grandma Ruby was clearly getting more flustered and anxious. All of a sudden she didn't seem to be her usual cool and in-control-of-everything self. Maybe it was the heat. I could feel the sun beating down, and drops of sweat were starting to run down my face. Frizz patrol! I pulled out my compact mirror to survey the damage.

Suddenly, in the sea of tourists from all around the world, I saw a man in a tropical shirt coming our way, holding up a sign with "Ruby and Katani" written in large, red letters.

"There he is!" I exclaimed, pointing Grandma Ruby toward the man with the sign.

Even above the honking cars and the chattering tourists I could hear her breathe a sigh of relief.

"Wonderful!" She seemed calmer as she grabbed my arm. We waved to him, and he rushed right over.

"I'm Selvin," he introduced himself as he greeted us, shaking Grandma's hand and giving me a hug and a big, friendly smile. He smelled like the sea.

As we were waiting for Selvin to bring his car around, I noticed a very tall man wearing a cowboy hat and a loud, colorful shirt standing to the left of us. He was carrying an important-looking briefcase. I got the strange feeling that he had been staring at us, but he quickly turned away when he saw me looking at him. I wanted to point him out to Grandma, but when I turned and looked again, he had disappeared into a limo. Must be somebody important, I thought. Maybe he was a local celebrity. That would be fun! I could tell Maeve all about my star sighting when I got home.

Selvin drove up in a van painted my favorite color, Tuscan gold. On the side was a drawing of a smiling woman with the same headwrap I had seen on the singers inside the airport. She was holding a tray with loaves of bread in her hand. Under the drawing were the words "Nana's Banana Bliss."

The drawing looked as if it had been done by an inexperienced artist, but the longer I studied it, I realized that the artist's intent was to make everything look homey and colorful. I quickly took a picture so that I could show my friend Isabel, who liked to draw. I suddenly felt a little homesick for the BSG. Charlotte, Avery, Maeve, and Isabel were my best friends at home, and everyone called us the BSG—short for the Beacon Street Girls. They were so excited for me to come here, and now I wished they were here too.

Selvin put our bags in the back of the van, and we quickly got in beside him in the front.

"Welcome to Jamaica!" he announced in a funny accent. We both smiled, but by this time I was beginning to feel a little overwhelmed by the bright sunlight and my colorful, tropical surroundings. Everything seemed to scream color—the black, green, and gold of the national flag, the green of the trees, the brightly painted buildings on the hillside overlooking the airport, the sparkling blue of the sky—and after the winter drabness of home, my eyes weren't coping with this overload very well. I was happy to pull out my shades. With a lurch and a chug, we were off—driving through the tropical paradise . . . on the wrong side of the road!

"Oh!" Grandma Ruby exclaimed. "I forgot that you drive on the left here. It seems a bit strange."

Strange, all right; more than once I felt her pressing down on imaginary brakes.

"First, we going to look for Aunt Faith," Selvin explained.

"How is she?" Grandma asked quickly. Aunt Faith, Grandma had explained to the family before we left, was having eye surgery. She was in her seventies, so the surgery was kind of a big deal.

"Coming on. She get over the operation yesterday, but they keeping her till next week. You know, exercise her so she not get too stiff and test her eye till it heal. She's in Cornwall Regional Hospital. Is not visiting time, but Nurse will let me in, especially when I tell her you just come from America. We can't stay long, but she so excited to see you."

"I can't wait to see her, too," Grandma replied. "I've wanted to meet her in person for so many years." Was it my imagination, or did her voice sound kind of choked up?

"Your time is so short, you not gwine get to see plenty things. So I will be your tour guide as we drive along." He laughed. "We will stop on the way home for lunch. You ever eat jerk pork?" he asked.

"My mother spoke of it, but I've never tasted it," Grandma murmured.

"You gwine love it."

Selvin's accent was strange to my ears. Grandma Ruby had explained to me before we left that Jamaicans spoke English and a patois (which she pronounced "paTWAH"), which was a little like English but a bit more musical sounding. He spoke slowly and although I knew he was speaking English, sometimes I missed a word or two and had to guess what he was saying. One thing was for certain, though: I wasn't quite sure that I wanted to eat something called jerk pork. I was a pizza and mac-'n'-cheese girl myself.

I looked around, trying to take in my surroundings in the city center of Montego Bay. It was pretty lively—all the street sounds were like music, and the town was crowded with people and cars. The roads were really narrow, and the vehicles were driving so close together and to the people that it was amazing we didn't hit something or somebody. More than once I wanted to yell, "Look out!" but Selvin seemed to know exactly what to do . . . which was twist and turn and honk!

The streets were jammed with shops and other small businesses. I felt like I was in a colorful play village.

2. Montego Bay: an amazing color palette of sights and sounds. Saw a woman on the street wearing a wrap dress in a tropical print—SO "Island Chill"! Definitely more hip than Boston.

Soon we started climbing a steep hill where there were fewer buildings spread wider apart. When the hospital, a large multistory building, came in sight, I thought it looked drab and kind of scary on its perch on top of the hill. I was beginning to get nervous. Where were all those famous Jamaican beaches? I wanted to put on my bathing suit and jump into the warm Caribbean Sea. I'd read online that people sometimes said the seawater was like swimming in warm bathwater. After five-degree weather at home, warm water sounded dreamy.

Selvin drove through what seemed to be a back gate and parked. The guard didn't even stop him. He just nodded, lifted the barrier, and waved us through. He obviously knew Selvin.

By Name and Nature

"We'll just go through the service section," he said. "I can't bother argue with the security in front."

He led us through a side entrance, past a large, busy kitchen, where he waved to some people. "We need some Bliss, Selvin. When you gwine bring it?" shouted one of the cooks.

"Soon, mon, very soon. Don't worry," Selvin answered, as he directed us to follow him up some stairs. We passed several wards, climbed even higher, and I was just beginning to wonder if he knew where he was going when he stopped at a room marked "Surgery Recovery." He pushed through the heavy doors and led us to a desk at which a big, grumpy-looking nurse was sitting, writing in a book. She informed us sternly, "Visiting hours are over."

Then she recognized Selvin and raised her eyebrows. "Oh, it's you." *Does my cousin know everyone in Jamaica?*

"Morning, Sister," he responded respectfully. "Just a few minutes. They just come off the plane. We won't stay long, I promise." "Sister"—is that what they called nurses here? Boy, was my notebook going to be full when I got home. My friends were not going to believe how different things were in Jamaica.

"Few minutes," she warned him. "The doctors are due any minute now."

Selvin then led us into a ward with a lot of beds. Some of the patients were sleeping. Others looked at us curiously as we walked down the aisle to about the third row. Selvin stopped beside a bed where an older woman lay. The head of the bed was raised a bit, and she looked as if she had been reading the Bible that was in her hands. One of her eyes had a black patch over it. Funny thing was, her other eye was closed behind her glasses. She must have nodded off.

"Aunt Faith," Selvin said gently. "Them come."

She opened her eyes, looked confused for a moment, then focused on Grandma Ruby and me.

"Is you that?" she asked in a voice shaky with emotion. "Is it really you, Ruby?"

"Yes, Aunt Faith, it's me. How're you feeling?"

"Good! Good. Good. Better, now that you come. Come, give the old lady a hug."

She stretched out her hands, which were wrinkled and frail, and Grandma leaned over and hugged her. I couldn't believe a lady this old was running her own business. Then I saw that Grandma's eyes were wet. A single tear rolled down her cheek. My always-in-control, very cool, positively unflappable grandmother was melting before my eyes.

There was a box of tissues on the small table beside the bed. I handed it to her, and she took out one and dabbed at her eyes.

"Just call me Faith—by name and nature." The old lady smiled. "'Aunt' is for the young ones. And this must be Kantani," she said, stretching out her hands to me. I also gave her a brief hug.

"Katani," Grandma pronounced my name correctly for her.

I didn't quite know what to think or say, so I settled for just a "Hi!"

"She's tall, just like my Olivia," Aunt Faith observed, as she looked me up and down. Olivia was my cousin, and I was really looking forward to meeting her. Now I was extra curious to see what she looked like.

"I know you can't stay long. Selvin and Cousin Cecil will show you everything, and I write out everything you need to know. I so glad you could come. We need to keep that Bliss coming," Aunt Faith said as she handed Grandma Ruby a paper filled with her spidery scrawl.

"We make it back Sunday," Selvin said. "Everything all right?"

"Yes." She waved away his concern. "Just a little weakness. I getting good care. I getting better. I don't even know why them keeping me so long, till next week. Gertie come every day and look after me. She will call you if I need anything. You gwan, and take good care of Ruby and Katani." She got my name right this time. "Olivia and Enid are at the house," she told us. "They show you everything."

She was staring at Grandma as if she couldn't get enough of her. "You favor Mama, you know. Same forehead and nose."

Grandma Ruby grabbed Aunt Faith's hand, and Aunt Faith brought her close and whispered in her ear for a few moments. I saw Grandma nod several times and smile. I didn't want her to be sad, so I gave her a big hug when she walked beside me. I guessed that it might be very emotional to see a relative for the first time, one you thought you might never meet.

Several of the patients had been showing great interest in our little reunion. They smiled and nodded at us as we passed. I didn't want to be rude or anything, so I nodded back at all of them. I felt bad that they were all in the hospital when outside, the sun was shining, the sky was blue, and the beaches were, I was sure, completely awesome! I suddenly wondered how anybody got any work done in this country.

"'Member to feed them!" Aunt Faith called after Selvin. "My niece and her granddaughter. They come from 'Merica to . . ." I heard the pride in Aunt Faith's voice as she explained who we were to the woman in the bed next to her, but we were quickly out of earshot and I missed the rest of what she said.

The nurse nodded at us as we passed her desk. I was glad to escape outside. I hated the smell of disinfectant. Medicine was definitely not in my future.

3

Montego Bay Surprise

We had just left the hospital gate when a professional-looking van passed us and stayed in front of us until it turned left at the next corner.

"That's one of Mr. Biggs's vans," Selvin announced, just before the van turned the corner. I looked closely at the vehicle driving away from us. It was a covered van like ours, but much bigger. It was also painted yellow. On the back was a fancy drawing of a man in a chef's hat. The words under the drawing read "Manteca Bay Bakery Company. Try Mr. Biggs Better Banana Bread." Somehow the man in the drawing looked familiar to me. But how could that be? I had never been to Jamaica before.

"He has some nerve!" Grandma Ruby exclaimed as she frowned. "Who tells him it is *better*. Better than what?"

Whoa! Chill, Grandma! I had never seen her get mad so fast. It was just banana bread, after all.

"Him sell other products too," explained Selvin, "but for some reason, he has decided he want to push out Aunt Faith completely and get our Banana Bliss name. He's big and we're small. I don't know why him won't leave us alone." Selvin pounded his fist on the wheel. He sounded as angry as Grandma Ruby. I guessed banana bread was a big deal in Jamaica.

Selvin drove onto a street he called the famous Hip Strip, home to the world-famous Doctors Cave Beach, which was about five miles of white sand on the edge of the cystal clear sea. *Finally! Now we're talking.* "Can we stop now? " I asked hopefully. "Just for a minute?"

Selvin shook his head. "Home is a good distance away," he explained, "but we can stop at a place called Scotchies for lunch, if you want." As he said the word "lunch," my stomach growled. I hadn't realized that I was so hungry. I hoped they had burgers and not that weird jerk pork he'd mentioned earlier.

With my nose pressed against the window, I could get a clear view of everything, including all the luxury hotels and beaches. I closed my eyes for a minute and imagined a waiter serving me a lovely cold drink in my lounge chair on the beach. I would, of course, be wearing my new Tuscan gold tankini and my straw hat. I could even feel my bangle bracelets lightly jingle on my arm. After all, a girl has to keep her own sense of style, wherever she is.

It was getting warm in the van, so I stuck my face out the window just like Marty. As the official mascot dog of the BSG, the "little dude" assumed that position whenever we took him for a ride. I chuckled to myself when I suddenly envisioned Marty dressed in a Hawaiian shirt and riding a surfboard. As we passed a beach, I almost screamed out loud for Selvin to stop. I couldn't wait to get into the inviting blue water. I waved sadly as we raced by the turquoise sea.

Don't Be a Jerk!

Selvin drove into a small, enclosed area with two open booths under thatched roofs. A group of tourists were sitting at round wooden tables in front, eating food out of foil paper and licking their fingers. Was this a restaurant? It looked more like a campsite to me.

On the other side was a long wooden bench running the length of the wall with some wooden tables placed in front of it. A group of construction workers were sitting on stools at a bar chatting loudly as they sipped their drinks and tapped their feet to the reggae music playing in the background. I could get used to this, I thought.

"All right!" Selvin exclaimed, rubbing his hands together like he was getting ready for a serious feast. "We have jerk chicken, jerk pork, and fish, so you can taste all of them." A man brought over some drink bottles for us. "That's coconut water," Selvin explained.

"Sounds delicious," I answered. "I'm sooo thirsty!" I opened my bottle and took a long, cool taste. Frankly, I was a little disappointed because the taste was mild and kind of flat. I would have rather had a soda, but I didn't want to say anything to hurt Selvin's feelings.

When our food arrived, I figured I better dig in before my stomach made a giant, obnoxious gurgle. I still wasn't sure about meat called "jerk," but I squeezed my eyes shut and took a tiny bite anyway. Whoa! It was totally delish! The jerk chicken and pork had the texture of roasted meat. Both were very highly seasoned and really tasty. I ate the whole thing in what seemed to be a minute. I couldn't wait to tell Avery about Jamaican jerk barbecue. Maybe she would tell her brother Scott, who was an amateur chef, and he might make a little jerk just for the BSG.

"If you pour the hot pepper sauce in that little paper cup over the meat, you get the true Jamaican flavor," Selvin explained. Was it just my imagination, or was he trying really hard not to laugh? Whatever. I thought a little sauce sounded great. So I poured just a little of the sauce on my plate, dipped a piece of the meat into it, and chomped down.

Yikes! You know those cartoons where you see fire coming out of people's mouths?—that's how it felt. My eyes started watering and every nerve ending in my mouth started screaming as I grabbed the coconut water and tried to quench the burning sensation. A boy at the next table started laughing. Selvin grinned. "You'll get used to it," he assured me, pouring a big glop of the sauce on his chicken! *Yeah*, I thought, *just when my taste buds have been scorched beyond repair*. I wished I had a big bowl of strawberry ice cream in front of me. Grandma Ruby must have read my mind, because she jumped up and came back from the counter with a Popsicle. I was never so happy for something cold in my entire life.

Lucky for her, Grandma was a little more composed than me, although I saw her sneaking frequent sips of the coconut water too.

Saltwater Cowboys

As we drove along the north coast road toward Aunt Faith's home, we kept passing more and more resorts, and everywhere there was a spectacular view of the sea. I was practically drooling. If I didn't get to a beach soon, I was going to have some kind of attack. "Grandma," I begged, "couldn't we just stop for a minute so I can put my feet in the water? I just want to feel the sand between my toes and the warm sea on my skin. I'm dying here!" I knew I was being kind of dramatic, but geesh, I had traveled 1,700 miles, and I was in Jamaica!

Before Grandma Ruby could give me the raised eyebrow, Selvin answered, "Oh, Katani, we cannot have you dying here in Jamaica! This place is for living. I know a beach you will like. It is

"As we drove along the north coast road toward Aunt Faith's home, we kept passing more and more resorts, and everywhere there was a spectacular view of the sea."

not too far." He winked at us, and I looked at Grandma Ruby.

"Well, this *is* a vacation," Grandma agreed, breaking into a grin.

We hadn't driven too far outside Montego Bay when Selvin pulled off into a parking lot with a sign that said "Island Cove Adventures."

"I have some good friends here," Selvin explained. "You like horses, I think I have heard, right, Katani?"

Like horses?! Riding was the first sport I had ever shown any skill whatsoever at, and I completely loved it.

"Yes, definitely!"

"Here you can ride them in the ocean, right on the beach. How does that sound?"

I could hardly believe my ears. "It sounds wonderful!" I exclaimed. "Thank you!" Beaches *and* horses, all in one—it was like this Island Cove place was custom-designed just for me.

Before I knew it, I was saddled on a huge bay named Lazarus. Only instead of real saddles like I was used to at home, here they used a spongy pad that could go in the water. Everyone else in my group was still mounting, but as soon as I held the reins, Lazarus started to trot away.

One of the attendants raced up on a horse. "Pull up! Pull up!" he shouted. I pulled on the reins, and Lazarus stopped.

"You're a rider, lady," the man said. I thought he was asking if I knew how to ride, so I nodded.

"That's why him want to run. Them can feel somebody with experience."

I smiled and sat up a little straighter in the saddle as Joe, the leader, took my group down to the beach. As soon as we entered the water, the attendants started yelling, "Yah! Yah!" and racing around, trying to get the horses to go faster.

It was such a rush galloping through the water! I could feel the pull of the water against my legs and hear it swishing against Lazarus as he galloped through. I felt him straining to push through the water and go even faster. "Good boy," I whispered, patting the side of his neck.

Joe led the horses in a line, and we galloped through the water around and around the cove. The horses weren't really in that deep, because the cove was pretty shallow. I only got wet to my waist. I stroked Lazarus's neck as we moved through the water together. I thought of Penelope, the horse I rode at home. I wasn't sure if pretty Penelope would like splashing around in the water with all these other horses and people laughing and yelling. She was a prim-and-proper Boston girl all the way. But then, so was I—and I was having a blast!

The ride ended way too soon. "Can we please stay just a little longer?" I begged Selvin and Grandma Ruby as I dismounted. "Just to lie out on the beach for a little while?"

Selvin shook his head. "Got to get home. Olivia will be wanting to meet you." I wanted to meet Olivia, too, but it was still sad to say good-bye to Lazarus and the beautiful beach.

"Come visit me in Boston, okay, Lazarus?" I whispered to the huge horse. He gave a snort and a toss of his head, almost like he was nodding yes!

Our Jamaican Home

Back in the car, Selvin kept up a running commentary on all the places we passed. "There is Columbus Park." He pointed at a tiny museum on the sea. "It marks the spot where they say Christopher Columbus landed in 1494." Wow. It was kind of exciting to drive by the same place where Columbus had landed.

We drove for a while through lush green countryside, and now, instead of the sea, I was surrounded by what looked like farms with tall trees full of coconuts and lots of banana trees with their bright green leaves drooping like long, broad fans, gently waving in the breeze. Then I noticed something weird: All the bunches of very green bananas on the trees were covered in blue plastic.

"What's up with the plastic?" I asked Selvin.

"It protect the fruit while it grows," Selvin explained. "Most of these bananas will ship to Europe. Buyers won't accept the bananas if they are bruised."

That made sense. It seemed like people were very careful with bananas here, treating them like gold. I saw a woman walk by balancing a tray of bananas on her head and I snapped a picture through the window. Charlotte would love it. She'd lived in lots of different places and always said it was so interesting to see how people in other countries lived.

All of a sudden I realized that we were going up a really steep hill. Who knew Jamaica had mountains? I looked back and noticed that the ocean was getting very small. I had a moment of panic. Was I ever going to be able to go to the beach again? I had imagined that we would always be close to the water, where I could get a quick dip before the end of the day. After all, Jamaica is an island, right? Just a speck in the Caribbean Sea. Now here I was in the middle of some mountain. I sat back in silence and I must have had a sulky look on my face, because Grandma gave me a look—the one that said, *I am watching you, so mind your manners. Now.*

"Not much farther now," Selvin commented as we passed through a sleepy looking village named Banana Ground. "We're almost there."

Finally he turned off the road onto a gravel track, lined on either side with banana trees, and then stopped in front of the house where we would stay. I got out and had to stretch the cramps out of my legs and back.

While he got our suitcases out of the cab, I checked the place out. The house was spread out, with a porch that Selvin called a veranda all around the front and sides. Like a lot of the other houses I had seen along the way, it was painted in a bright color—yellow (there was my favorite color again!)—with edgings of brown around the windows and doors. The walls were made of concrete, but the veranda had a wooden floor and railings.

In the yard, flowering shrubs and beds of roses surrounded the house. I took a quick photo and made a note in my Island Inspiration Notebook—I definitely wanted to remember all those colors to use in a sundress next summer!

Selvin blew the horn, and shortly after, a woman emerged at the right side of the veranda. Selvin introduced her as Enid, who helped take care of the house. She had big brown eyes and a pretty smile. She waved hello and took one of the suitcases and told us to follow her.

"Where's Olivia?" Selvin asked.

"It still early," Enid answered. "She don't come from school yet."

We followed Enid into the house. Inside, it was cool, which was a relief because it was super hot outside. The big living room had large, antique-looking sofas and chairs and a table to seat eight in the dining area. *Wow*, I thought. *This is way bigger than our dining room at home!*

"This Miss Faith bedroom," Enid said as she put Grandma's suitcase in a small room off the main room. She was showing me where I would sleep, on the other side of the house, when we heard running footsteps and a girlish voice asking, "They come long time?"

"We just reach," Selvin's voice answered, and a girl dressed in what had to be a school uniform entered the house and threw her backpack on a chair.

"Hi," she said as she spotted me. "I'm Olivia. And you must be Katani."

CHAPTER

4

Olivia Style

O livia greeted me with a big hug and hello as if we were old, long-lost friends. She seemed so friendly and self confident. I could tell right away that this girl (just as tall as me!) was totally comfy in her own skin—definitely not afraid to be herself, wherever she was.

I'm usually kind of reserved about making new friends. At school I have a reputation for being a little hard to get to know, or standoffish, and it even took me some time to accept Isabel when Maeve wanted to include her in the BSG. But with Olivia, it was different. I instantly felt close to her. I had heard Grandma once say that families feel connected in ways they don't even understand. I don't know if that's why I warmed to Olivia so quickly—because she was family?

She took me to her room, which I would share with her for my stay. Like all the others in the house, this room was large but didn't have much furniture—just two small, mis-matched beds, a dresser, and a writing desk and a chair. On one wall was a large, framed picture of Olivia as a little kid and a pretty woman I guessed was her mom. Grandma had told me Olivia's mother had died a few years ago. On another wall there were several papers taped up. They looked like charts and school projects and lists.

Olivia ran to the closet and pushed her clothes to the side, making room for my stuff. "Go ahead, hang anything you want in there. Do you want a drawer, too?"

"Sure!" I told her. She was being so nice, moving all her things around for me. As I lifted some clothes out of my suitcase, I spotted a new headband I'd bought just before I left Boston. The tag was still on it and everything.

"This is for you," I told Olivia, holding out the headband. I knew that Grandma Ruby had brought gifts for the whole family, but I wanted to give something of my own to Olivia. "Thanks for sharing your room and your family with me."

"Oh, thank *you*!" she exclaimed. "I'll be wearing this to church on Sunday. It'll match my dress."

She changed from her uniform into what she called "home clothes"—faded jeans rolled up to capri length, a faded, big, light blue T-shirt knotted at the side, and old, not very clean sneakers. Definitely not high fashion, but that girl wore her clothes with confidence! Style must be in the family genes.

Looking at Olivia's outfit, I suddenly had a lightbulb moment about the difference between fashion and style, and I dug out my notebook to write it down.

4. Difference between fashionable and stylish:
Style comes from inside a person.

If I had thought about it before I'd come to Jamaica, I would have imagined that I would be the one making an impression, with my foreign clothes and my signature Kgirl look. But I had nothing over this girl, I could tell.

Olivia tied her head with a cloth. "To keep my plaits neat," she said, "while I do my chores." After a confused second, I realized "plaits" meant "braids." I practically needed a dictionary to keep up with the way people talked around here!

Goat Herding?

"Oh, no thank you," Grandma Ruby was saying to Enid as Olivia and I walked into the kitchen. "Katani and I aren't very hungry. Selvin took us for a big lunch."

Enid smiled. "But you must be thirsty. Come, drink," she commanded us. Enid was one of those people you don't say no to, so we followed her to the back of the house, where there was a giant pile of coconuts. Suddenly, from out of nowhere, she pulled out the biggest knife I'd ever seen! Yikes! Before I could spit out a question, Olivia saw the surprised look on my face and smiled. "That's called a cutlass," she explained as Enid chipped off the tops of a few coconuts and invited us to drink the water out of the husk. I guessed I was going to have my fill of coconut water today!

I hadn't really liked the bottled coconut water at Scotchies, but drinking it straight from the fruit gave it a much better flavor. When we were finished drinking, Enid split the husk with another ginormous knife.

"Go on now, eat the jelly," Enid invited us, holding out the husk of the coconut. She explained that the jelly is the part of the coconut that becomes hard and white when it dries. It looked sort of like soft, colorless Jell-O. It had to be scooped out with a "spoon" cut off a side of the husk, and I felt very awkward scooping it out. Olivia laughingly showed me how to do it, then invited me to go with her while she tended her goats. Goats?

My eyebrows shot up. This was definitely not what I expected from my Jamaican vacation! What about a dip in the sea or a nice nap under a palm tree? Hanging out with a bunch of goats was definitely not my cup of tea, but Olivia was already out the door. This was the first thing she asked me to do with her, and I didn't want to be rude. Grandma Ruby gave me a reassuring nod. "Go with Olivia, Katani," she encouraged me. So I followed Olivia outside.

The goats were in pens some distance from the house. Along the way I saw a hen and some small chickens scratching in the dirt. They ran away as we came closer. "The goats are my project," Olivia explained as we walked. "When we sell one of them, my father puts the money into an education fund for me. I want to be a vet, since I plan to own my own farm. You have to know how to take care of the animals properly."

I couldn't believe we were alike in so many ways! I mean, living on a farm is definitely not in the Kgirl life plan (and I leave all that animal stuff to Avery), but I also know what I want to do when I leave school. I want to become a fashion designer and own a chain of stores especially for professional women. I've been saving my money earned from baby sitting and selling hand-knit scarves to start a college fund. I wanted to tell Olivia all about it, but as I jumped aside to avoid another squawking chicken, I decided that right now I had to concentrate on this vacation. It just kept surprising me.

I am strictly a city girl, so this farm life was kind of freaky. I mean, I love riding horses at High Hopes Riding Stable, back in Boston, but I also like being able to take a walk over to Irving's Toy and Card Shop for candy and Think Pink! for the latest fashions. I was already feeling weird as I followed Olivia on the path through an untidy growth of tall grass and what had to be weeds, some of which were leaving green stuff clinging to my jeans.

"Leave them until we get back to the house," Olivia advised when she saw me trying to brush them off. "They'll come off easily enough." *Good thing I'm in a strange country,* I thought. *None of my friends can see the Kgirl disintegrating into a fashion disaster.*

"Say hello to my goats!" Olivia greeted them when we arrived at their pen. The goats acted like they were Olivia's pets, running over to the fence so she could scratch their heads and pat them. Some of the BSG had guinea pigs, a snake, and other weird pets . . . but no one had goats. Then of course there was Marty, that we all share.

There were six goats, mostly a drab brown color and ordinary-looking creatures —except for one. That one was brown, with large, dirty white spots, long, floppy white ears, horns curling backward, and BIG! He reached Olivia above her waist. In fact, I thought for a minute that he was a calf. Olivia said, with great pride, that he was an Anglo-Nubian goat, a special breed. She called him Spotty.

I didn't like the look of Spotty one bit. When we entered the pen, he stood beside Olivia and stared at me as if he were inspecting me. The pen gave off a sharp smell that made me wrinkle my nose. P-U! At first, I wasn't really afraid, but that goat stood looking me up and down and suddenly I began to feel that if he didn't approve of me, I would have to get out of his pen—fast.

Olivia laughed when she saw the expression on my face. "That Spotty thinks he owns the place and everything in it. You can't come near his goats unless he approves of you. Isn't that funny?" She turned her attention back to the goat and talked in that weird, baby-talk voice people sometimes use with their pets. "It's okay, Spotty," she said as she rubbed his head. "This is Katani. She came all the way from America." Then she turned back to me, still laughing. "Katani, meet Spotty."

I gulped. Was that goat glaring at me?

"Hi, Spotty," I said, feeling like a total dork. I mean, I wasn't used to talking to goats.

Spotty stared at me for a moment. *Uh-oh*, I thought. Now he was definitely glaring at me. "Um, Olivia?" I started to say—when suddenly Spotty bowed his head and started charging right toward me!

"Ahhhhh!" I shrieked, racing toward the gate as fast as I could. I could hear Spotty's hooves pounding the dirt behind me.

"Spotty, stop! Come back!" I heard Olivia scolding him. But this goat was in no mood to slow down.

Just in time, I made it outside the fence and slammed the gate behind me. I heard Spotty skidding to a stop. I turned around, panting, and saw Olivia laughing so hard, she was about to split a gut.

Now I was really annoyed. "Well, I don't think it's very funny!" I said, trying to catch my breath. Me, the Queen of Cool, running away from a goat! This Jamaican adventure was not going the way I had imagined.

Olivia immediately stopped laughing when she saw I was serious. "I'm sorry, Katani," she apologized. "Him just wild sometimes. Wait over by the trees, I'll be right out."

So Where's the Beach?

While I waited for Olivia to finish up with the goats, I tried to regain my composure by looking around a little.

There sure were a lot of banana plants. Selvin had told us that they had a couple acres planted in bananas. Most of the trees had bananas on them, and the bunches of fruit were covered with the same blue plastic I had seen before. At the roots of the trees there were other young ones shooting up.

When Olivia came out of the pen, she noticed me looking at the trees. "When the fruit is ready, those on the left are sent to the packaging plant for export to Europe," she told me. "Aunt Faith uses the fruit from the trees on the right to make her Banana Bliss. They are special and have a nicer flavor than the others. That's why Banana Bliss tastes so good."

All this stuff about goats and bananas was interesting, but after my near-death experience with Spotty, all I wanted to do was find some warm sand and a cold fruit punch. "So when are we going to the beach?" I asked Olivia.

"I don't know," she responded. "The beach is far from here, but I suppose Cousin Selvin will arrange something." That didn't sound very promising at all.

Banana Bliss

By the time we got back to the house I was completely exhausted. My head was spinning from a long travel day and an overload of sun. I wondered if my body actually knew I had traveled to another country and was telling me to chill.

Lucky for us, Enid had prepared some cool lemonade and slices of Banana Bliss. I was super curious to taste it, since that was what had brought us to Jamaica in the first place. The loaf of bread looked like a firm, golden cake with tiny streaks of black.

A little table had been set on the side of the veranda closest to the kitchen. On it were jars of guava jelly, honey, and a small butter dish. Enid explained that we could eat the banana bread without anything on it or we could spread it with the jelly, honey, or butter.

"Banana bread can eat all sorts of ways," Enid went on. "It can eat like bread or cake, so you can eat it by itself, or you can eat it with egg and cheese and plenty other things."

I decided to try it with the guava jelly. Grandma spread honey on hers. Enid, Selvin, and Olivia were looking at us closely as we bit into the Banana Bliss. I guess they were anxious to see our reaction the first time we tasted it. My taste buds danced when I took the first bite. This stuff was fabulous! The guava jelly just made it even better. No wonder Banana Bliss was popular. "Wow!" I said to show my appreciation. "This *is* bliss!"

"It's really wonderful," Grandma Ruby murmured with a delighted look on her face. Olivia and Selvin and Enid nodded at each other, satisfied at our reaction.

"This one is a few days old. The last batch Aunt Faith made. Wait until you taste it freshly baked," Selvin promised. "We bake every other day, so tomorrow morning bright and early, we start baking again. I'll come for you by five o'clock, so set your alarm. Baking takes about three hours, then they have to be cool before they can be wrapped, and I start deliveries about ten o'clock. Okay?"

Grandma nodded. I got the impression that she couldn't wait to get into the bakery. She loved baking, AND she was going to show Mr. Biggs who had the best banana bread on this island.

CHAPTER

5

Getting to Know You

I decided I needed to lie down and rest for a few minutes, but when I opened my eyes it was dark out. I must have slept for a couple hours at least. It must have been the Jamaican heat, because at home I never took naps. I managed a big cat stretch before dragging myself off to the bathroom, where I splashed cold water on my face and looked in the mirror. Aaaagh! I almost had a heart attack. My hair was sticking out in little spikes all over my head—kind of like a porcupine. Hair gel to the rescue! With all the humidity down here, it was going to be tough to keep a decent style. I patted my frizz down with some water and gel and went to find Grandma Ruby.

I poked my head around the corner. Where was everyone? There was no light at all in the house, which made it feel kind of creepy. I was no fan of things that went bump in the dark, so I searched for the light switch in the living room and flicked it on. Then I went out to the veranda, where I saw Grandma fast asleep. A notebook she had been reading had fallen off her lap. It had the same spidery handwriting I had seen in the letter back home: Aunt Faith's writing. It was the instructions for baking Banana Bliss. Grandma must have been studying it.

As I flipped through the pages, Grandma sensed my presence and opened her eyes.

"Grandma, where is everybody?" I asked.

She took off her glasses and wiped her eyes. "Good gracious," she said. "I nodded off. Are you all right?"

"Fine," I replied. "I had a good nap too. Where's Olivia?"

"She said something about choir practice at church. I think Selvin might have taken her. I don't know where Enid is." Then she saw the notebook in my hand and gently took it away.

"Do you know that Aunt Faith has a secret ingredient in her banana bread? She inherited the recipe from her grandmother. That's why she calls it 'Nana's Banana Bliss.'" She waved a folded piece of paper at me. "I'm supposed to memorize the secret ingredient and destroy the paper." She laughed like a little girl. "I feel as if I'm in one of those spy movies. Maybe I *should* swallow the paper, just in case Mr. Biggs tries to get hold of it."

I groaned. Here was Grandma Ruby threatening to act out a Maeve movie fantasy. My friend Maeve could make a drama out of a trip to the grocery store. I missed that redhead, even though she and I didn't see eye-to-eye on organization. Traveling with Maeve was like traveling with your own personal cyclone—clothes and shoes and stuff swirling every which way. Maeve as a roommate could be an overwhelming experience.

All of a sudden, a big truck drove into the yard and parked at the side of the house. The man fiddled around in the cab for a minute, then climbed out, carrying a battered old briefcase, and looked around. He saw us watching him and waved.

"That must be Cecil, Olivia's father," Grandma Ruby whispered, waving back to the man. "You should call him Cousin Cecil. It's a sign of respect here not to call older people by just their first names. My mother taught me that."

Cousin Cecil didn't look like a farmer. He was dressed in khaki pants and shirt and looked more like a supervisor-type. As he strode up to the veranda I noticed that he had a very determined walk, almost like he was an army general or something. And, just like the rest of my family, he was super tall.

"So sorry I couldn't be here to welcome you," he said in a deep voice. "Busy day getting bananas to the packing house. I hope they took care of you."

He shook Grandma's hand. When it was my turn, I felt like I should almost curtsy or something! He definitely wasn't as friendly as Selvin, and I wondered if perhaps he hadn't wanted us to come. Maybe Grandma Ruby and I would have to check into a resort—one on a beach, of course. I thought I would ask her about that later.

Fishy Business

Dinner was okay, although I got the feeling Cousin Cecil was really anxious about making a good impression on us. More than once he got on Olivia's case for something he thought she had done wrong. Obviously, since Aunt Faith wasn't around, he expected Olivia to take her place and be the perfect hostess. She didn't seem to be bothered by anything he said, though, and chattered away about Jamaican foods. She must be a good cook, I thought, because she seemed to understand a lot about spices and what went with what.

For dinner, we had fried chicken, fried fish, and rice cooked with red beans, which they called rice and peas. There was also boiled yam and green bananas, and home-baked macaroni and cheese that looked seriously yummy. I noticed that Olivia wasn't eating any chicken, and when I asked why, she said that she didn't eat meat.

"She don't know what she missing. Half her life gone, and she so young. Poor thing!" smirked Selvin in mock sorrow.

Cousin Cecil glared at him, and I began to think that Cousin Cecil was mean and that maybe I wouldn't like him very much. My dad was the jokester type, so I wasn't quite sure how to handle somebody so serious.

"My mom was vegetarian too." Olivia sounded sort of quiet, and suddenly I didn't feel like eating any more chicken either.

"My wife died three years ago," Cousin Cecil said gruffly. It was kind of obvious to everyone that that would be the end of that conversation. I concentrated on the fried fish, which was spicy and vinegary. Escoveitch fish, they called it. It was pretty tasty. I made a note to tell Avery about this because she loved fish.

"Cecil," my grandma asked, "how long has your family been farming bananas?" Thank goodness for Grandma Ruby, because grumpy Cousin Cecil suddenly turned into a talk show host and started giving us the whole history of the farm and how important bananas were in the island economy. My Kgirl business sense perked up. It was fascinating to learn what it took to get a bunch of bananas to market. What it took was a lot of hard work and money. I couldn't stop myself from saying, "Boy, people shouldn't really complain about how much bananas cost in the supermarket." Cousin Cecil seemed to agree and nodded approvingly.

When we were finished, Selvin helped us clear the table. Once, when he and I were in the kitchen, he pulled me aside and whispered in a low voice not to mind Cousin Cecil. "He used to be very pleasant, make plenty joke and thing, but him get a bit touchy since his wife died," he explained. I could understand that, but it didn't make it any easier to deal with him.

Grandma Ruby waved off dessert, which was a custard smothered in coconut-flavored cream. How could she do that? She insisted on sipping her coconut water instead. Big mistake. The custard was, to quote my mother, "simply delightful."

Grandma and Cousin Cecil went to sit on the veranda while the rest of us washed the dinner things and put them away. No dishwasher here. Water was piped in from a large tank at the back of the house. I was learning the lay of the land fast. Selvin made things really fun by singing reggae tunes, and Olivia and I danced around the kitchen. I showed her some of Maeve's dance moves, and she showed me some local Jamaican moves. How cool would I be back in Boston?! I could teach all the BSG some Jamaican dance styles when I got home.

Afterward, Olivia and I went to watch television, but almost right after we turned it on, all the lights went out. "Ooo!" Olivia wailed in a funny voice. She made a spooky face, and I was forced to throw my pillow at her when she wouldn't stop. Major pillow fight. We were laughing so loud that we failed to see Cousin Cecil standing in the doorway. "Olivia, "he voiced sternly. "You shush now and stop all this silliness." My feelings for Cousin Cecil just got worse. I was going to have to talk to Grandma Ruby about whether it was the right thing to do to hang out here for our whole vacation.

Once Upon a Time . . .

"Power cut!" Selvin exclaimed as Olivia and I walked into the living room.

"We got a big wind out there," announced Cousin Cecil as he quickly lit two lamps. They were weird, old-looking kerosene lamps with the words "Home, Sweet Home" written on the shades. He put one in the living room and one in the kitchen.

"Are we having a hurricane?" I asked nervously as I heard the shutters rattle.

"No, no, Katani," Cousin Cecil said in a softer voice. "Just a little Caribbean wind. It come sometime. Nothing to worry about."

I looked up at him and thought I saw the beginnings of a tiny smile. My cousin was very confusing. Sometimes nice, sometimes grumpy. Cousin Cecil was definitely going to take some getting used to.

"I was going to town, guess I pass now." Selvin complained. "I don't know what a gwine happen with dem lights."

"Well, I for one find the wind very relaxing," said Grandma Ruby as she headed back out to the veranda. We all followed her and sat outside in semidarkness.

Beyond the house it was very dark. Every now and then I could see little flickers of light flying around. "The fireflies are pretty," I commented to Olivia.

She laughed. "Girl, we call those peenie-wallies."

Then it was my turn to laugh. "Peenie-wallies," I repeated.

The words people used in Jamaica were definitely fun.

Whenever we were quiet, I could hear the strange noises of night creatures. Olivia told me what they were. Croaking lizards—ugh! An owl or two! Crickets and tree toads! I hoped they kept their distance. Meeting Spotty was enough wildlife for me in one day. Once, I thought I heard something like a big animal moving through the banana trees, which were not very far away.

"Do you have any . . . any . . . like, wild animals in Jamaica?" I asked.

"You mean like lions and tigers?" Selvin laughed. "No. Not even monkeys. It's only if Spotty get away."

I shuddered at the idea of Spotty being loose. "Doesn't he get locked up?" I asked.

He and Olivia collapsed with laughter, but Cousin Cecil told them to behave, as if Selvin were also a child. "I'll tell you some other time. Not tonight," Cousin Cecil replied.

Olivia and Selvin kept snickering. Obviously I had asked something silly. Maybe Spotty was an escapee or something.

"Dad, since there is no TV, why don't you tell us one of your stories?" Olivia asked.

"Yes," Selvin agreed enthusiastically. "When you don't have no light, you tell Anansi story, or . . ."—he paused to snicker—"Spotty story."

Olivia began to sing, and Selvin joined her.

> "Moonshine tonight
> Come mek we dance and sing
> Moonshine tonight
> Come mek we play ring ding."

Whoa! Olivia could really sing! Selvin was singing a sort of second part, and then—I could hardly believe it—Grandma joined in.

"Me deh rock so
You deh rock so
Under banyan tree
Me deh rock so
You deh rock so
Under banyan tree."

I am pretty sure my mouth was open in surprise.

"You know that song?" I asked Grandma.

"My mother used to sing it for me when I was a little girl." She sighed, and there was that choked-up sound in her voice again. "I remembered it when they started singing."

I think Cousin Cecil understood that it was an emotional moment for her. "Well," he said. "There's no moon, and it's a long time since I've told any Anansi stories. . . ."

"Not since Mom died," Olivia whispered to me.

"Who's Anansi?" I asked.

"Him a spiiiiiider," Selvin answered, wiggling his fingers in my direction and making a goofy face. Olivia and I both burst out laughing.

"They say all the stories in the world belong to Anansi," Olivia explained when she caught her breath.

"I'd like to hear one," Grandma joined in encouragingly.

Cousin Cecil thought for a minute. "Well, now. Let me see. I know a story that doesn't have Anansi in it, but I think it's one that ol' spider would like. . . ."

"The River Mumma," by Cousin Cecil

"In Jamaica, we don't have a lot of big rivers. You can go rafting down the Martha Brae in Trelawny, or on the Rio Grande in Portland, and boats can travel for a distance on the Black River in St. Elizabeth, but that's probably it. Most of the rivers are quite small. In the rainy season, of course, they can become raging torrents, but generally they just run quietly, minding their own business. Some of them, though, do have places where the water is like a large pool, and these can be very deep.

"In the rural areas, some villages don't have piped water, so water is fetched from the river to do daily chores. Usually that's the children's job when they are old enough, especially the boy children, since they are stronger.

"Most times, the boys in the village would go to the river at the same time each day, have a swim, play a game or two or just chat, before returning home with their buckets of water. This is Orrin's story."

Orrin was a young man living in one such village. Although they owned a few acres of land, his family was very poor. He and his father farmed the land without much success. He was fed up with his life and wanted to run away to the nearest city where he thought he would be able to make a better living. Since he had no brothers and sisters, there was no one else to go to the river and that remained his task, even after he left school. He had outgrown going to play with the other lads, so now he went alone, usually around midday, when few people wanted to walk in the hot sun to fetch water. Often he sat on the bank of the river fretting and wondering how he could make his life better.

One day, he was feeling particularly sorry for himself. He sat by the riverbank, bucket at his feet, wishing there was some way he could get his hands on some money. If he had some money, he could buy fertilizer for the crops; he could get better tools and hire help and plant more crops.

He could see it in his mind's eye: a thriving
farm, his father sitting on the veranda, feeling good,
and perhaps presents for everyone in the family.

Orrin sighed as his foot kicked the bucket and
he came back to reality. He picked it up wearily, then
paused. Out in the riverbed, there had been a flash of
brilliant light, much more brilliant than the sun.

What could it be? He rubbed his eyes and looked
out into the middle of the river where the sparkling
water flowed deep blue and peaceful. Then he gasped.
There on the rock . . . there, sitting on the large rock
in the middle of the water . . . could it be . . .

"River Mumma!" cried Selvin, startling all of us. I had
been so wrapped up in the story, I was almost surprised to
find that I was still on the veranda in the semidarkness.

"That's what country people call a mermaid," Olivia told
me, in a soft voice.

"Thank you very much," Cousin Cecil spoke sternly.
"May I continue?"

I sighed and sat back in the chair. Yikes! Cousin Cecil was
so uptight.

"Please do," said Grandma Ruby.

Yes, it was a River Mumma, or, as Olivia
explained, a mermaid. Now all his life, from when he
was a little boy, Orrin had heard about this fabulous
creature who lived in the depths of the water. Every
now and then she would come to the surface, sit on
a rock, and comb her long hair with a golden comb.
If something frightened her and she left the comb
behind and you found it, you would have to return it
or she would call your name forever until you came
and returned the comb.

❉ 40 ❉

Orrin had always believed this was just another folktale to amuse children, but here she was in living color, sunning herself on the rock and combing her long, long hair. Her back was to him, so he couldn't see her face.

He was so surprised that the bucket fell out of his hand and clattered against the river stones. Quick as a flash, so fast he could barely see her movements, the River Mumma dived into the water. But Orrin saw that she had left her comb behind. It shone and sparkled and glittered with a thousand different rays from the gold and jewels with which it was made.

He wasted no time. Quickly he waded through the water; then, as it got deeper, he swam to the rock and retrieved the comb. Back on the bank, he turned it over and over in his hand. A few strands of the River Mumma's long hair were stuck in it. He took them out, folded them carefully and put them in his shirt pocket. He couldn't believe his good luck. The comb must be worth a fortune, he thought. It was deco- rated with a lot of beautiful gems; rubies, diamonds, emeralds. Though he had never seen jewels like these before, he knew that what he had in his hand was almost priceless. This was the answer to all his prob- lems. He would take it into the city and sell it to a jeweler. He was sure he would get enough money to make a better life for himself and his father.

"He didn't remember that she would call to him forever?" I asked, then put my hand over my mouth as I realized I was interrupting.

"No," Cousin Cecil answered. "He was dazzled by all

those jewels. He forgot about the legend that said the River Mumma would come back for her comb and would call to him until he returned it."

Suddenly, the electricity returned, and we were bathed in the bright light from the veranda bulb. Blinking, we looked around at one another, as if we had been in a different world and were suddenly pulled back to this one.

"Right!" Cousin Cecil said. "That's enough for tonight. I'll continue the story tomorrow night."

"Oh, no!" I groaned. "I hate cliff-hangers. Now I'll be thinking about what happened to Orrin all night long."

"Please, Dad, you can't leave us hanging," Olivia begged. "I never heard that one before. It's still early."

"Tomorrow night," he promised. He had returned from being the mysterious storyteller to his usual stern self. "Besides, I want to have a little chat with Ruby before she turns in."

An Invitation from Olivia

"Your dad is quite a storyteller," I remarked to Olivia when we were getting ready for bed. "I bet he could go around to schools and everything. Kids love those kinds of tales. You know—the ones that are a little scary, but not too much," I explained as I climbed under the covers.

"Yeah," she replied. "My mom used to tell him she was going to start collecting his stories and get them published. He stopped telling stories after she died. Tonight, he was *almost* like his old self. Good thing you came. Him used to laugh a lot before. Maybe him laugh more now."

Poor Cousin Cecil. I had never lost anybody close to me, and I didn't even want to think about such sad things.

I wasn't feeling sleepy, and neither was Olivia, it seemed.

This was a chance to get to know her better, so I asked her about her school.

"I love school!" she said. Her enthusiasm for everything kept reminding me of Maeve. "We have a three-day holiday from school this week. And on Monday, we're celebrating Black History Month. My class is making a presentation on Marcus Garvey. You know who he is, right?" I shook my head. "He's one of our national heroes!" Olivia explained. "He grew up in Jamaica more than a hundred years ago, and then he moved to New York to fight for civil rights. Anyway, I'm in the class presentation. You should come," she told me. "My friends would love to meet you."

I thought about it for a moment. Going to school on my vacation wasn't exactly what I had pictured for this trip, but it might be kind of interesting to see what school was like in another place.

"Yes!" she said, clapping her hands and raising her fists in the air. It was a gesture I would see her make whenever she was excited or very happy about anything from then on.

Just as I was about to close my eyes I thought of Spotty and laughed out loud. "Are you crazy, laughing in your sleep?" she teased.

"I'm just thinking about that crazy Spotty," I told her.

"He's quite harmless," she assured me. "Him just bumptious and show-off." Olivia moved easily between English and patois. But I noticed that around her dad she only spoke English. Selvin and Enid also spoke patois. My ear was getting a little used to their pretty accents and I could mostly follow what they were saying without asking them to repeat too often. Soon I fell into a deep sleep with the sounds of patois, a vision of the River Mumma, and Olivia's singing in my head.

CHAPTER

6

Making the Rounds

When I woke up the next morning, bright sunlight was streaming through the open window as I was remembering a lovely dream about blue water and shells and pretty little fish swimming around my ankles. It took me a few moments to realize that I was in Jamaica at my Cousin Cecil's farm, high up in the mountains . . . far from a beach.

Olivia's bed was already made and I heard sounds and smells coming from the kitchen, so I quickly made my bed and got ready for the day. I decided to wear my favorite tie-dyed T-shirt and my cutoff jeans. I also slipped on a pair of gold hoops. I mean, just because I was staying in the country didn't mean I couldn't glam up a bit.

As I fried my frizz head with a straightening iron, I wondered why Grandma Ruby hadn't woken me up, until I remembered that Selvin had said he would pick her up at five o'clock to take her to the bakery. It was way past that, I was sure.

I went into the kitchen, where Enid was stirring a pot on the stove. "Good morning," I greeted her. "Where is everybody?"

"Olivia say to tell you that she soon come. She gone look

after the goats. When she come, you will eat breakfast. You want some tea?"

I told her I would wait for Olivia. I hoped she wouldn't be too long, as I was starving. I went onto the veranda and looked around. We were too far from the road for me to see anything, but I could hear vehicles and now and then loud talking as people went about their business. Lots of selling and talk of bananas going on. A little gossip here and there about some woman who sounded mean. Guess there were Queens of Mean everywhere. In my school we had Anna and Joline—those girls had nothing good to say about anybody.

When Olivia came in, she was deliriously happy. One of her goats, Lily, had given birth to two kids. She had put them into a smaller pen away from the others.

"How's Spotty?" I asked sarcastically.

She grinned. "He's okay. I keep the kids away in case he gets any funny ideas. He's a strange one. Once, he wouldn't allow anyone near the kids, even the mother. Don't know what that crazy goat expected those babies to do."

She went to change her clothes, and then we sat down in the kitchen to a breakfast of boiled green bananas and salted mackerel cooked in coconut milk with lots of onions and tomatoes and pepper. Enid called it "run down." All the meats here were cooked with a lot of seasonings. There was also a hot drink they called "chocolate tea"—a thick, muddy kind of cocoa. I didn't much care for this breakfast. I really wanted cereal, or a nice big piece of Banana Bliss, but I tried to eat enough to be polite.

I could hear Grandma's voice in my head saying, *Katani, at least try what's being offered.* Grandma Ruby was definitely old-school about manners and things. But fish for breakfast? Hello! I couldn't wait to tell Charlotte about this. She'd be impressed that I actually took more than one bite and didn't utter one word of complaint. Charlotte said if you were going to be a world traveler, you had to be open to all sorts of new things. Even things that seemed a little yucky or weird.

Just as we finished eating, Selvin drove up. "Ruby could use some help now," he announced. "You can come with me when I am making deliveries later. And wear your swimsuits underneath," he added mysteriously.

At last, I thought. Beach! My kind of action!

Bakery Bliss

Aunt Faith's bakery was about a mile away from the farm. I was kind of shocked when I saw the home of Nana's Banana Bliss. You know how you can imagine things and then they turn out to be way different? I guess I was thinking it would be like Montoya's bakery back home. Not even close.

The Bliss Bakery was a rectangular, bright turquoise brick building, narrow in front and long at the sides. Inside, there was no place for customers to sit and enjoy the baked products like at Montoya's. Selvin saw my look of disappointment and explained: "This strictly a place where they bake Banana Bliss. Then we drive all the Bliss to the fancy resorts. The customers eat it up." He laughed at his own joke.

As we walked in, Olivia pointed out Selvin's house—a small cottage over on the side. "Aunt Faith used to live here too, until my mom died, then she came to live with us," Olivia told me.

"Where's Selvin's family?" I whispered to Olivia as soon as I was sure he couldn't hear. I had been wondering about this for some time.

"His wife and son migrated to England to be with her

family after they divorced," she whispered back. "He save up so his son can come here once a year."

"How come they got divorced?" I asked, even though I knew it wasn't any of my business. But I really liked Selvin and wanted to know.

"His wife just miss her mother and family too much. Selvin tried to live in England, but he said there was never any sun and the people didn't smile too much, so him come back to Jamaica to help Aunt Faith and my father."

As we entered the bakery through the front room, I saw that it was a kind of office with two desks—and a computer! I couldn't wait to ask permission to use it to send a message to the BSG. They must be wondering what had happened to me. They would never believe that I had been in Jamaica for a whole day and I still hadn't been swimming! I didn't think the horseback riding counted. But first I wanted to see if I could grab a slice of Bliss. The sweet smell of banana was driving me wild.

When we entered the oven section of the bakery, I let out a huge hoot. Grandma Ruby was covered in flour dust, from the plastic cap on her head to her plastic overshoes. Even her eyebrows looked floury. Lucky I brought my camera—this memory was a keeper. Everybody at home was going to love seeing Grandma Ruby as the Baker Lady of Jamaica.

"I'll clean up later," she joked when she saw me gaping at her. "A bag of flour burst all over me." Then she started laughing. Soon everybody in the bakery joined in. If only the kids at Abigail Adams Junior High could see their principal now.

"Whew!" she exclaimed. "What a morning! It's going to be short." She nodded to Selvin. "We lost some time cleaning up the flour disaster."

Grandma Ruby made a mistake?! She caught my surprised look. "Yes, Katani, your grandmother is capable of messing up . . . literally messing up," she said, and she blew some flour off her shirt.

"No problem," Selvin said with a smile. He was a very easygoing person. "I'll just deliver to the customers we really can't afford to lose. No worry," he added. "It will get easier."

Grandma Ruby frowned, and I couldn't tell whether it was because she wasn't sure it would get easier, or because she thought she should have gotten it right from the beginning. That was probably it, since she was a perfectionist. And I was just like her. I hated making mistakes too. I went over and gave her a hug because I know that's what she would have done for me. She leaned her head on my shoulder and hugged me back. It was then that I realized for the first time that I was almost as tall as she was. Wow, I must have grown this year without even knowing it.

Two women helped wrap the breads and put them in boxes that Selvin then loaded inside the back of the van onto racks. Each box held about ten loaves. I guessed there were two hundred loaves in all. That seemed like a lot, but I wasn't quite sure.

Then Grandma Ruby introduced me to her helpers. One was Miss Gloria, and the other, a much younger woman, was called Precious. They nodded at us and continued their work. Miss Gloria kept tapping her watch. She obviously wasn't interested in any idle chitchat. "Precious, dem customers need their Bliss. We got to get a move on." It was clear that people were very serious about business in Jamaica.

I asked permission to use the computer to send a message to the BSG, and Grandma Ruby said it was fine. It took a while for Olivia to make the dial-up connection, so it had to be a very short note because Selvin was ready to leave.

```
To: Maeve, Isabel, Avery, Charlotte
From: Katani

Hi, BSG,

Just getting a chance at the computer.
Reached Jamaica safely. Going to beach
soon with my cousin Olivia, nearly
same age as us. Just saying hi to let
u know I'm OK. So much to tell u! Met
an aristocratic "bumptious" goat who
doesn't like me. LOL. Sorry, Maeve, no
cute boys yet. More later.

—Kgirl
```

A Bit of Jamaica-style Shopping

We soon arrived in Ochi, which is what Jamaicans call the town of Ocho Rios. While Selvin delivered Banana Bliss to the distribution depot, Olivia and I went to the gas station to get a soda to go with our warm slices of Bliss that Precious had snuck to us before we left. The place was super busy, with small and large tour buses and taxis and private cars zigzagging everywhere. There was even a cruise ship in the port, one so big it looked like a gigantic apartment building floating in the water. "Olivia," I said, sighing, "doesn't that ship look so glamorous? Can't you just imagine all the beautiful people dressed up in fancy dresses and dinner jackets?"

"Girl"—Olivia looked at me like I was crazy—"the sun has gone to your head."

"Maybe." I laughed. I realized that I was beginning to sound like Maeve, who loved all things romantic and fancy.

Suddenly, Olivia spied two of her school friends and called them over. They skipped across the street, dodging cars and taxis, and she introduced us. We chatted for a little while—I mostly listened, because they were talking in patois so fast I couldn't keep up. Olivia told them I would be coming to their school on Monday. As they were leaving, they reminded her about the green blouse for her costume.

"Help!" she exclaimed. "I completely forgot. And Aunt Faith is not there to make it for me. What am I gonna do?"

If I'd had a sewing machine, Grandma Ruby and I could have helped her in a second. But not having a solution, I shrugged.

"I'm going to have to buy one today," she decided. Happy day! That meant I would get a chance to go into the stores. I couldn't wait to get a look at the local styles.

We went looking for Selvin, who gave her some money and told her to be as quick as possible. We crossed the road, which was a death-defying exercise because there was no pedestrian crossing and traffic was wild—cars honking and lots of people pulling out in front of one another. A couple of people yelled at us, but Olivia just grabbed my hand and zigzagged us across the road. Good thing Grandma Ruby wasn't around for this scene. I breathed a sigh of relief when we reached the other curb.

As we ducked in and out of shops I pulled out my Island Inspiration notebook and started taking notes.

Some of the stores carried large pieces of cloth that could be used as headwraps. Everything was brightly colored, lots of green and red and purple and yellow flowers and birds, and these amazing abstract designs on the materials. I saw a piece of cloth in the black, green, and gold colors of the flag and thought it would make a fabulous skirt.

"It hopeless to try to find anything here!" Olivia finally declared. "I'll ask Selvin to stop at one of the little towns on the way."

Selvin wasn't happy about stopping before he started his other deliveries, but he was sympathetic about Olivia's problem, so in the next town we stopped in a side street.

On the sidewalk was a man dressed all in white. "He's a Rastafarian," Olivia whispered when she saw me staring. His head was wrapped in a high turban, to hold his dreadlocks, I supposed. His loose, long-sleeved shirt hung to below his knees, like a short gown. His pants were baggy, and he wore sandals. His beard was thin and kind of ragged. Around his neck, hanging to waist length, was a sash to die for. It was intricately woven in the red, yellow, and green Rasta colors, with a shiny gold border ending in a fringe, which glistened softly when the sunlight caught it. He looked very regal, like someone from another time.

"Broom, Princess?" he asked in a very polite voice as I paused to look at him. "Jah-Jah order this one specially fi you." He held out a roughly made straw broom.

"No thanks," Olivia replied as she took my arm and drew me away.

"Respect," he replied in a resigned tone.

"He's a bobo dread," she whispered. "They live in the hills and make and sell the best brooms on the island, but we already have enough brooms."

Olivia was getting anxious to find her shirt so we headed into another store. Finally she found the almost perfect shirt in the perfect color green. It wasn't exactly what she wanted, but she said that if the collar were cut off and the neckline lowered, it would work.

"Olivia," I told her, "I can def fix this for you. A little needle and thread and you'll have a completely new shirt." I do a ton of sewing at home, so I wasn't too worried about the job.

The Patty Wagon

Selvin had bought us something called "patties" and fruit drinks before we started our delivery rounds. I was practically drooling from the yummy smell. He had bought three beef patties—two for himself and one for me to taste—as well as three callaloo patties, two for Olivia and one for me. Callaloo is like spinach with smaller leaves. Earlier they had showed me some in a basket that a woman on the sidewalk was selling.

My first taste of a Jamaican patty! Scrumptious! A patty looks like a half-moon-shaped turnover, but the crust isn't as flaky as a turnover's, and it's filled with a spicy meat or vegetable stew. Selvin explained that at first you could only get beef patties, but now they were made with a variety of meat fillings and different vegetables. A patty and a drink was a regular lunch for many Jamaicans, he explained.

"You should come to American and open up a Jamaican patty factory!" I told Selvin in between bites. "You'd make a fortune."

Selvin smiled but answered emphatically, "Jamaica is the place for me. Why would I want to be cold?" He had a point.

We delivered boxes of Banana Bliss to a few of the luxury hotels along the coast. It was fun carrying the trays into the fancy resorts. Some of them had little carts you could ride around in. I wished I could just run down to the beach and stay, but Selvin said I should be patient. "That's a lot to ask, Selvin, when you have come all the way from Boston, where it is so freezing cold, icicles grow off your nose!" I giggled.

Finally we arrived at a big hotel where Selvin said he usually got a large order. When we drove into the delivery area, Olivia and I couldn't believe our eyes. There was a Mr. Biggs Better Banana Bread van unloading on the ramp!

"Uh-oh!" Selvin exclaimed. "Trouble!"

Olivia and I quickly got out of the van and followed Selvin. Two men in elaborate chef's hats were carrying trays of banana bread into the kitchen area. They looked very dramatic, as if they were in a play or something, I had to admit, the way they presented themselves was very impressive. Suddenly, I felt a major stab of concern for Nana's Banana Bliss. Mr. Biggs's group was pretty fancy.

"What's this?' Selvin asked the man who was receiving the bread.

"Hey, Selvin!" the man exclaimed. He was genuinely surprised to see Selvin. "We heard that Faith was sick and the business closed. No more Banana Bliss."

"Who could tell you that, Mr P?" Selvin asked.

Mr. P looked around embarrassed. He really didn't have to answer. It was obvious.

"So, you dealing with Mr. Biggs now?"

"Well, he offered us free samples, and we're trying it."

Aunt Faith and Grandma were going to be devastated. I could just imagine their faces.

"Okay," Selvin retorted. "Can't fight free samples. But I'm telling you, you'll be sorry. Your guests are going to notice the difference."

"Ah, well"—he turned to us—"they'll learn. No better-tasting thing than Banana Bliss." He winked at Olivia and me. "Come on, girls. I arranged with my friend for you to take a swim with the dolphins. Let me take you over to the main entrance. I'll try to get the rest of these breads sold to some other places while you have some fun. I should be back in about an hour or so. All right?"

"Hold up. Did he just say *dolphins*?!" I exclaimed.

"Yes!" Olivia said happily.

The BSG would never believe this.

CHAPTER

7

Dancing with the Dolphins

To: Maeve, Isabel, Avery, Charlotte
From: Katani
Subject: Dolphins!!!!

OK, BSG—I am sending this from one
of the most beautiful resorts in all
of the Caribbean. My cousin Selvin's
friend works here and she said I could
use her computer to send an e-mail—nice
lady. Yes! Well, get ready for this: I
just met up with some dolphins. Yup,
the Kgirl became a regular nature girl.
It was like I was in that old movie we
liked—the one about the dolphins that
talked. You remember, Maeve? From the
moment I sat in the golf cart that took
us down to the beach, it was like there
was someone saying, "Roll camera!" I
was the star (sorry, Maeve!), with my

cousin Olivia as my sidekick. Avery,
you would have loved it!

So check this movie out: As Olivia and
I ride through fan-tabulous grounds
with fancy cottages and people dressed
in resort wear, the camera pans to show
royal palm trees and gentle waterways
with spouts of water shooting into the
air. With my equally fan-tabulous Tuscan
gold tankini and big, white-rimmed
sunglasses, I'm just where I belong.
Enjoying the sun, I notice the perfect
blue Caribbean sky with a white jet
trail disappearing in the distance. No
snow and ice here. THIS PLACE IS TO DIE
FOR!

P.S. This has to be a BSG meeting place
someday—you know, like once a year, when
we're all grown up, we all fly in from
wherever we live and meet up for a week
of total bliss (like Banana Bliss, get
it?) in the Jamaican sun.

Let me continue with my movie: OK,
you can't see my eyes behind my cool
designer sunglasses (I got them at
Filene's Basement for five dollars—
righteous bargain, huh?), but my eyes
are wide open, recording everything
to my memory. We pass a man pruning a

tree, and he waves and smiles. We wave.
The driver calls out to him, "All right,
Bushy?" "Yes, I!" comes the answer. (Did
I tell you people talk way differently
here? I'll explain it when I get home.)

We stop in front of a stand that says
"Dolphin Lagoon," and we are welcomed
like royalty by the attendant, who
says we are just in time for the next
program. Olivia shouts, "Look!" In the
lagoon, two humongous dolphins rise from
the water, curve in the air, and dive
back in, just like in the real movie.
If only you were here, Ave! These things
looked ginormous. Much bigger in person.
Trust me on that.

Continuing on with Katani's Jamaican
Holiday, the movie: "Cut! Cut!" the
director shouts. The star def needed a
break. I have to decide, am I really
going into the water to swim with
those huge creatures? They must be
at least fifteen feet tall. I look
over at Olivia. She's super excited.
There's a huge grin on her face, but
she wants to be a vet, so this must
be great for her. Me? You all know how
I like to be in control, and these
dolphins look like they might like to
be in charge too.

"I have to decide, am I really going into the water to swim with those huge creatures?"

So the attendant says, "Hurry, girls! You don't want to miss a moment of this program." We head toward the beach, strip to our swimsuits, rub on the suntan lotion, and put on the life jackets.

I take a deep breath as Olivia and I hold hands and we all enter the water, led by three attendants. There is one in a kayak rowing out to a stand in the water. That's where we're headed. My knees are shaking.

We are in an enclosed part of the
beach, surrounded by rocks and mesh,
which is the dolphins' home. The water
is rippling from a light breeze, and
believe me, you need that breeze because
the sun is now right over our heads.
There are three seagulls sitting on the
rocks, checking out the whole scene and
probably waiting for a tidbit or two.

Olivia and I wade out toward the stand
where there are two trainers waiting
for us. Soon it gets too deep for
walking, so we start swimming out to
where the dolphins, Bruno and Miguel,
are already playing with one of the
trainers. Oh, yeah, here's what I'm
thinking: There better not be any
sharks in here!

The trainer waves his hands and
the dolphins are off, like circus
performers, jumping out of the water
in perfect unison, two or three times.
Before we're all finished exclaiming and
clapping, Bruno and Miguel are back at
the stand, collecting their reward. The
trainer waves his hands again, and this
time they walk backward on the water.
You almost can't believe they can do
such a thing.

"Cut!" the director shouts again. Oops!
Our heroine (me, the Kgirl!) is afraid
to get close to the dolphins. These
creatures are very frisky, and you can't
tell from one moment to the next where
they might be!

"It's okay." One of the trainers
notices me slinking behind Olivia, who
is very brave and can't wait to touch
these little darlings. "They are quite
friendly, and we are in total control."
Olivia takes my hand to reassure me as
I tread water.

The rest is like a total dream sequence.
I touch the dolphins (rubbery feeling); I
hold on to their fins and ride with them
a short distance (Eeeek!); I allow myself
to be kissed (my first kiss and it's by
a dolphin—ha-ha); AND then I, Katani Ida
Summers, dance with the dolphins.

At the trainer's instructions, we hold
our hands in the air and turn around in
the water as if we are dancing while he
beats on a pan and the dolphins dance
around with us, making their little
high-pitched squeak sounds. Fear Factor
is over. I'm having an incredible time!
All of a sudden the trainer starts to
sing, and those dolphins sing along

with him, just like they're in a band
(a squeaky/screamy kind of band) or
something. Then comes the big finale.

I watch as one of the trainers takes
one of the group apart, holds him
steady, and—oh, my gosh! The man is
flying out of the water, pushed by the
dolphins, and then, they just let him
down near the water's edge. I want to
clap and shake all at the same time.

Olivia goes next. She grins like a
madwoman as she goes flying through the
water. Then it's my turn. "Don't be
afraid. Put your feet behind you. Lift
your hands in the air," the trainer tells
me, and whoosh! Two snouts have connected
with the bottom of my feet (it tickles!),
and the dolphins are pushing me through
the water, my body and hands in the air.
So this is what it feels like to be
Superwoman and fly! "Cut and print"—this
scene is in my memory forever.

So what do you think, BSG? Ready for a
trip to Jamaica? Oops, I gotta go now—
Selvin and Olivia are waiting. But have
I got pictures!

Just as I was finishing up my e-mail, Olivia came into the
office with Selvin's friend and handed me a cold pineapple

punch, which I slurped down quickly. "I have to get Selvin to bring me back here again!" she exclaimed. I hadn't seen her get so excited about anything since I'd been here.

"You've never done this?" I asked with surprise.

"No. I always thought this was just tourist stuff. It's a good thing you came."

I thanked Selvin's friend for allowing me to use her computer, and Olivia and I went outside for the golf cart to take us back to the kitchen, where Selvin was waiting.

When we got back to the front of the hotel, Selvin was waiting in the parking lot for us. I couldn't help it. I rushed over and gave him a thank-you hug. This had been one of the best days of my life. The sun was out, the water was blue, and I had gone dancing with dolphins.

CHAPTER

8

A Daring Idea

ousin Cecil informed us that church started at nine o'clock
sharp on Sunday morning, but we all had to be there very
early because Olivia's youth group would be leading the
service.

Back in Brookline, we don't dress fancy for church, so I
figured my miniskirt with the little black and green circles on
it and the matching top with spaghetti straps would be hot
but cool, if you know what I mean. At home I get a lot of com-
pliments when I wear that outfit. Even my dad likes it, and
Isabel recently pronounced it "very groovy." I was twirling
around, examining the swirling circles in the mirror, when
Olivia came from the bathroom and saw me.

"Er, Katani . . . ," she began. From the expression on her
face I knew something was up. "Do you have anything a little
longer?" she asked.

"Huh?" What was she talking about?

"The church sisters . . . they don't approve of too-short
dresses in church. If you were a tourist, it might be okay, but
since you are family . . ."

"Church sisters? What?!" I exclaimed.

"Sister Lyn . . . she'll be giving you the scrutiny eye, and then everybody turns to look at you—it can be quite embarrassing, Katani." Olivia sounded very apologetic, but I could feel my temper rising. "Sister Lyn is kinda old; some of the sisters say she may be even ninety-five. She's been in the church forever, so they just let her do what she wants," Olivia explained with a shrug of her shoulders.

I stared at my cousin with my hands on my hips and set her straight. "Olivia, I know this is your church and everything, but I have to wear what I think is best. I'm all about my style groove and I can't go by what other people think. You know what I mean?" I wanted Olivia to understand that I didn't mean to be disrespectful or anything. It's just that a girl has to have her standards.

But Olivia wasn't listening to me. She was looking behind me at the door. I stared back at Olivia, but I just knew Grandma Ruby was standing right behind me.

"Olivia, honey," Grandma said in a very polite voice, "can you please give Katani and me a few minutes alone?" Olivia gave me one of those sympathy looks—the kind that says, *Sorry, can't help you out.*

Okay. So, after a lengthy discussion with Grandma Ruby about respecting the customs of Jamaica, I had to rethink my whole outfit. Lucky for me I had also brought my blue dress with cap sleeves and a flared skirt that ended just a bit below my knees. Of course, I then had to change my shoes—it was all so totally annoying. I really wanted to wear the miniskirt, but that was that.

Olivia came back in wearing a pretty plaid skirt with pleats starting below her hips. I had the perfect top for her, in the exact coral shade of one of the colors in the plaid. When I showed her, she happily switched the shirts. I love it when I can help someone make a snazzy outfit.

Olivia was so excited about her new outfit that she hugged me. "Oh!" she shouted suddenly, pulling back from me and looking like a lightbulb had just gone on over her head. "There is a necklace in my mom's jewelry box that would be just right to go with this."

She left the room for a bit and came back looking flushed. "Good thing my dad wasn't in his room so I could sneak it out."

"Should you?" I asked. Now I was the one who was nervous. What if her dad found out? I didn't think Cousin Cecil would be real chill about something like that.

"He won't allow me to wear Mom's jewelry. He says I am too young, but I think it's that he doesn't want to see anyone wearing her things. My mom would want me to look pretty. I mean, look, Katani, see how beautiful it looks with this shirt."

She was right about it being the perfect accessory. The necklace was handmade from small, flat, very smooth multicolored stones intermixed with delicate seashells. Olivia said that her grandfather had made it especially for her mom. He had spent a lot of time looking for the perfect stones and shells. Her mother had cherished it. "Really, Katani, I'm sure that my mother would want me to wear it," Olivia reassured me. I could see that although it couldn't be considered super expensive—I mean, it wasn't made of diamonds or anything—the necklace was a treasure. And I guessed that it had a lot of sentimental value, like it was priceless to the family.

"But, won't your dad see it?" I asked.

"I'll just hide it inside the blouse until afterward, and when we are with the other girls I'll show it off. Fasten it, please," she directed, turning her back to me. "No problem, I've done it before." I wasn't sure I believed her.

As I fastened the clasp, I totally had a bad feeling about her wearing the necklace. "Olivia, I don't . . . ," I started, but Olivia just turned around, admiring herself in the mirror. Then she tucked the necklace inside the collar of the blouse.

"My mom was a teacher," she said, her face growing sad. "She was quite a bit younger than Dad and very pretty . . . tall like you and me. He was so sad when she died. Really hasn't been himself since. That's why he gets kind of grumpy sometimes." She paused for a second. "He's getting better, though. He took me shopping last week, and we had ice cream. It was lovely," she added with a smile.

With a sinking feeling in the pit of my stomach, I followed Olivia out of the room and went looking for Grandma Ruby. "Whoa, Grandma, you rock!" I whistled. "You look absolutely fab!" She was wearing a light brown crocheted vest over a cream cotton shirt with matching crocheted sleeves, a striped skirt in different complementing shades of brown, and brown pumps. I had never seen that outfit. Tall is good for showing off clothes.

"Really," I added, "you are positively RADIANT." Now that was all Kelley, exactly as she would have said it. I suddenly felt homesick for my sister Kelley. She's mildly autistic, and she's always completely honest. It seems like she knows just what to say to make you feel really happy or sad. Kelley definitely took some getting used to, but she was priceless!

Grandma Ruby gave me one of her *You can't trick me* looks, but I could see that she was pleased. She reached up to fix the dark brown hat that was perched on her head, tilting it a little to the side so it looked super fashionable. "Do you like my hat?" she asked with a teasing look on her face.

I was tempted to reply, "No, I do not like your hat. Good-bye!" It was an old joke between us from the P. D. Eastman book *Go, Dog. Go!* But I couldn't. That hat was perfect on her silver hair drawn back into a sleek bun.

When we came out onto the veranda, Cousin Cecil was there waiting. He looked at us and nodded. I could tell he was pleased with the way we all looked, even if he didn't say so. I grabbed Olivia's hand and give it a squeeze as Selvin drove up.

"Mama!" he cried, when he saw all of us. We three smiled. It's nice to know that you're looking good.

The road to town seemed deserted except for those going to church. There were three churches in the area, Olivia explained, but she thought hers was the best. As we passed the churchgoers I realized that they really were all dressed up, and their skirts fell below the knee. I had to admit my blue dress was much more appropriate than a miniskirt. It seemed like church was a place to show off your best clothes. Some of the women wore hats in styles I had never seen. I had to bite the inside of my mouth to keep from laughing. Those hats were so baaad! One even looked like it had purple batwings coming out from the side.

Like Cousin Cecil, most of the men wore full suits, even though the sun already felt as hot as one of those big ovens in the Bliss Bakery. Selvin wasn't wearing a jacket, though. I figured that he, like Olivia and me, liked to do his own thing.

We parked the truck at the bakery, and Selvin left us briefly to go into his house for something. Then we started walking up the narrow lane to the church. "It's not too far," Selvin promised.

Olivia whispered in my ear, "When a Jamaican tells you somewhere is 'not too far' or 'just around the corner'—watch

❖ 67 ❖

out!" Sure enough, the lane was about a mile long, I hoped Grandma's shoes wouldn't hurt. She had "very delicate feet," which she was fond of telling us—a lot. I was glad I had put on comfortable sandals when I'd had to change my outfit.

We passed two small, rundown-looking houses before Olivia told me gleefully that the next house was Ol' Madda Bird's home. "Um, who?" I asked, completely bewildered.

Olivia slowed down, grabbed my hand and, lapsing into patois, whispered, "Ole Madda Bird, she blind. She come here long time ago. No one know where she came from, or anything about her." I felt a chill go up my back.

"Every day, all she does is sit on her veranda carving birds out of wood. She lives alone except for a little mangy dog that barks every time anybody passes her house."

"But how does she live?" I asked. "I mean, how does she get money and food and stuff?"

"Somebody comes and takes the birds to sell and brings her supplies and stuff. But nobody in the village really knows much about her," Olivia continued. "She has some of the birds hanging on the veranda. Wait till you see them. We think she is a witch."

"Olivia," I hooted. "There are no such thing as witches, girl."

Olivia giggled. "I know it, but you know, it's fun to be afraid sometimes."

We walked slowly, to let the adults get farther ahead. When we reached the house, which was set back a little way behind a ragged wire fence, Olivia bent down as if she were fixing her shoe, so that I could get a good look at Ol' Madda Bird. The shabby little wooden house was surrounded by bushes and seemed a little sad. The morning sun had not yet reached it, so it was in shadow. On the veranda were several wooden birds of different sizes, hanging from the ceiling, like an advertisement: "We like birds at this house."

Even from this distance I could see that they were very beautiful. Fortunately I had managed to squeeze my camera and my notebook into the fancy purse I was carrying, so I could snap a pic and scribble a quick note.

> 6. Bird carvings: smooth, with realistic-looking swirls for feathers. Eyes are glassy black and lifelike. Would swirls work on a sweater . . . with glassy black buttons? Tell Isabel all about this!

The birds swayed and spun gently in a little breeze and seemed to be looking around as if they were watching all that went on. I guessed that's one of the reasons why the children thought Ol' Madda Bird was a witch and were afraid of her. Me, I could hardly believe that a blind woman could carve so well. I wished that Isabel were here with me now so she could see the beautiful art this old blind woman was creating. Of all the BSG, Isabel would appreciate what it took to make these birds.

Ol' Madda Bird sat in an old wicker chair on the veranda. Her head was wrapped in a turban, and she wore a shawl around her shoulders even thought it was already about ninety degrees. She was carving on a piece of wood in her hand. She must have sensed that we had stopped and were staring at her, because she raised her head and seemed to look straight at us through her very dark shades and called out, "Who is it? That you, Olivia?"

My mouth dropped open. How did a blind lady know it was my cousin? Immediately we heard barking, and coming around the house was a small, black and white, scruffy-looking dog.

"Run!" Olivia said, and for the second time in two days I found myself running away from an animal. This vacation was turning out to be way different from what I'd expected—first a banana war, and now an old witch.

We slowed to a walk before we caught up with the adults, who had already entered the churchyard. Cousin Cecil looked at us suspiciously, but Olivia murmured, "I have to go," and quickly left us to join her group. "Thanks!" I yelled after her. Both Cousin Cecil and Grandma Ruby stared at me like they knew something was up. I just put up my hands and said, "What?" like nothing was wrong.

Alleluia!

In Brookline, we attend the Episcopal church, which they call "Anglican" in Jamaica. Our service is very formal, with everybody sitting and listening politely. Olivia's church was like a different planet! Everybody stood and swayed while the choir sang a bunch of lively gospel songs. And there was no passion organ here—the music was played on a keyboard, with two guitars and a drum set. This way it seemed more like a concert than a church service! I loved the way the music got everybody moving and singing. The youth choir led some of the singing, and they were really good. *You go, girl!* I thought with pride, watching Olivia do her thing at the center of the group.

I didn't know any of the songs, so I mostly kept quiet,

but they repeated them several times and since the words were projected on a screen we could all see, Grandma Ruby soon joined in, just like on the veranda at Cousin Cecil's house. It seemed she was determined to participate in every little bit of this experience of being in Jamaica. I was content with just clapping. I didn't want to subject anyone to the horribleness of my singing voice. Once, when I was singing at a sleepover back in Boston, my friend Avery grabbed two pillows and clapped them to the sides of her head. It was that bad.

When the pastor welcomed new faces, Selvin nudged me. Grandma was on her feet almost instantaneously, and I slowly rose up next to her, feeling embarrassed. Everybody in the church was staring at us as the pastor introduced us as relatives of the Palmer family. The crowd clapped and murmured about us, and Grandma looked around and smiled graciously. No doubt about it, she was enjoying herself. I could see Olivia grinning at me from the choir, and I tried to stand up straight to make a good impression on everybody. Good thing I was wearing that blue dress.

Then, a big surprise came for everyone. "We have another very important visitor," the pastor announced, "who has made a generous contribution to our expansion fund. Will you stand up, Mr. Biggs?" *The* Mr. Biggs?! I heard Grandma's sharp intake of breath. The church clapped loudly as he stood up with his back to us, and I angled my head to try to get a better look at him. He was a thin, tall man and looked very imposing in a light brown suit.

When he finally turned around to face us, it was my turn to gasp. It was the same tall man in the cowboy hat I had seen in the airport! Had he been spying on us? What a nerve that man had, trying to get the secret of Banana Bliss. I saw

Grandma Ruby had on her Queen of England look, which made me put my head up as well.

The choir began singing again, and I tried to forget about Mr. Biggs and Banana Bliss and the cowboy hat, instead, focusing on the music. Olivia had some solo parts. I was so proud. That girl had a voice as big as Texas! When the choir did a number that was accompanied by congo drums, they sang the chorus in the patois to a reggae beat:

> *"Ah fi mi pickney dese*
> *Ah fi mi pickney dem*
> *Mi mek dem in mi image*
> *Mi love dem and look out fi dem*
> *Ah fi mi pickney dese."*

I had no idea what they were singing, but the choir had the whole church rocking and singing together. There was a standing ovation and loud applause at the end. Afterward, we had to greet a lot of family friends and church folk. When I met Sister Lyn, I understood what Olivia meant. She was very old, bent over, even, but that woman could talk. She asked how long we were staying, then told Grandma everything she needed to see and do while she was in Jamaica. I could barely conceal my smile at hearing someone else ordering my grandma around.

I thought I was going to have to pick my jaw up off the floor when suddenly Mr. Biggs marched over to us. Did he really think we'd talk to him after everything he'd been trying to pull? But then, even more surprising, Grandma acknowledged his greeting in the most polite manner.

"How do you like Jamaica?" he asked in a hearty voice.

"It's beautiful," Grandma replied coolly. "Everything is perfectly lovely."

I covered my mouth and suppressed a giggle. Grandma

Ruby sounded like some fancy Englishwoman.

He bent toward her and lowered his voice, but I could still hear what he said.

"If you really come to help Faith, your only choice is to advise her to sell the bakery to me. She is getting too old and shaky. She knows she can't keep it open much longer, so she may as well sell it now. You know, I'm offering her a very fair price . . . a very nice price. I am a fair businessman, after all."

For once, Grandma was speechless. Before she could recover, he bowed to her, put on his cowboy hat, and walked away. Because of his height and size he was already conspicuous. The cowboy hat was a bit much. If I were his fashion adviser I'd say, *Mr. Biggs, lose the hat*.

"Did you hear that?" Grandma asked me. Her eyes narrowed, and I knew that her fighting spirit was up. "We'll see about that, Mr. Big Man," she said softly.

9

The Case of the Runaway Necklace

Just then, I saw Olivia beckoning to me from where she stood with a group of her friends. As I neared them, I heard a girl's spiteful voice saying, "So the barrel come. You get new blouse and headband."

The speaker and another girl put their heads together and started whispering and giggling.

Oh, no, I thought. Another set of Queens of Mean, just like Anna and Joline at Abigail Adams Junior High. Were they, like, *everywhere*?

Olivia just smiled at them, then she put her hand inside her collar to pull out the necklace and make them even more envious. Her face went pale. She turned to the side and patted the rest of her blouse frantically. Where was it?

My heart began to sink. She beckoned me to follow her and, when we were out of earshot, she said in a very frightened voice, "I can't find it. What will I do? It loss!"

"You're sure?" I asked. I also patted her skirt just to

see if the necklace had slipped off and gotten stuck in her clothes.

"What I gwine do?" she wailed softly. "If Daddy ever finds out . . ."

I was beginning to panic also. "Let's think," I said. "When was the last time you felt it?"

"I don't know." She looked like she'd just lost her best friend. We were quiet for a minute, then she snapped her fingers. "It must have dropped off when I bent down and Ol' Madda Bird's dog chased us away."

"Oh, my gosh!" I exclaimed. "That must be what the dog was doing! When we were running away, I looked back and saw him sniffing something in the road."

"Oh, no! Suppose he mash it up!"

"Let's go look."

"We can't just go like that. It will look suspicious. Let me think," she told me, and began pacing in a circle.

I tried to look around calmly, but I was feeling guilty. Maybe I should have tried harder to stop her. I felt even worse when I remembered that I was the one who had fastened the necklace. Maybe I hadn't fastened it correctly, and that's why it fell off. I wished the BSG were here. We could put our heads together and figure out what to do. What a mess!

"I got it," Olivia exclaimed, interrupting my thoughts. "Daddy has to stay back to secure the offering. He is the church treasurer. I'll tell him you want to send an e-mail to your friends, and we'll get the bakery key from Cousin Selvin and go on before them. Most of the people gone already, so we can peep into Ol' Madda Bird's yard and see if the necklace is there. It must be there! If someone had picked it up on the road, they would have announced it in church."

All I wanted to do was go home, put on my bathing suit, and go lounge on the beach. I was not cut out to be an FBI agent looking on a Caribbean island for lost necklaces, let alone a special family heirloom.

We lingered on the road before Ol' Madda Bird's house, peeking over the fence, trying to spot the necklace. Suddenly Olivia grabbed my hand. "See it there. Right on the top step. The sun shining on it. Oh, no! How're we going to get it?"

I noticed the "we" and my heart sank even further. Just then a couple walking from the church reached us.

"Something wrong, girls?" the man asked.

"Oh no, Brother Percy," Olivia answered quickly. "My cousin Katani come from America was just admiring the birds."

That girl could give Maeve an acting lesson or two. She was a natural.

When the couple was gone, Olivia breathed a sigh of relief. "I'm sorry about the lie," she said, looking up as if she was praying, "but I'm desperate."

Ol' Madda Bird was not on her veranda, but the dog came out through the open front door. It didn't bark but stood looking at us, cocking its head from one side to the other, then it went and stood over the necklace as if to say, *Gotcha!* We knew we didn't stand a chance trying to enter the yard to retrieve the necklace without making a huge stink, so we just walked by like we were minding our own business. I thought I heard an old woman laughing, but when I turned around, there was no one on the veranda. First Mr. Biggs. Now Ol' Madda Bird. My trip to Jamaica was turning out to be more than a beach vacation, that's for sure.

To: Avery, Charlotte, Maeve, Isabel
From: Katani
Subject: Bad news!

I don't have time to enter the chat
room, so I'll just give you a quick
update. Am on the way from church.
Olivia's in trouble with her mom's
necklace. She borrowed it without
permission, and now we have to figure a
way to get it back out of the clutches
of an old blind artist with a crazy
dog. This is BAD! Will tell u more next
time. Wish u all were here to help us
out of this jam.

—Kgirl

As we came out of the bakery we saw a blue SUV parked a little way down the road. Precious, who worked in the bakery, was beside it talking with the driver, and I suddenly realized that the man behind the wheel was Mr. Biggs. Now, why would Mr. Biggs be talking to Precious? Olivia was so worried, she didn't seem to have noticed anything. Precious got in the car and they drove off right before Grandma and the others came around the bend. This was seriously suspicious.

When we were back in the van, everybody started complimenting Olivia on her singing, but they must have noticed how subdued she was. Once or twice I saw her father looking at her closely. The whole situation was so tense I wanted to bite my nails into little stubs, but I resisted and tried to act cool. Good thing I have a lot of practice with that sort of thing.

Back home, Olivia and I changed into casual clothes and ate lunch. We were going to the hospital to visit Aunt Faith and take some of the rice and peas and chicken to her. Grandma Ruby took one of the Banana Bliss breads she had baked for Aunt Faith to taste. I noticed her fidgeting with the container she put the bread in, trying to make it just right. She seemed really nervous about what Aunt Faith would think of her bread. I opened my mouth to tell her about Mr. Biggs and Precious, but then shut it again—I didn't want her to have to worry about anything else.

10

Spies and Lies

An old woman was seated beside Aunt Faith's bed when we reached her.

"My goodness. I was just saying that you were all too busy to come out," Aunt Faith commented, but she seemed delighted by our visit.

She introduced the woman as Miss Gertie, her friend who lived in Montego Bay. "What I tell you," she said to Miss Gertie. "See, Katani and Olivia are almost the same height. And them favor each other too."

Olivia and I looked at each other as we barely contained our laughter. Although we were both tall, Olivia and I were as different as the red beans and gungu peas Enid sometimes cooked.

"I think I'm prettier, though, don't you think, Aunt?" Olivia joked.

Everyone had a good laugh at Olivia's fresh remark. I gave her a pinch and told her, "Payback will occur later."

Miss Gertie made way for Grandma Ruby to sit beside Aunt Faith, who held on to Grandma's hand as if she would never let go. Grandma gave her a slice of the Banana Bliss she had baked—her first attempt. Everyone waited to see Aunt Faith's response. There was silence for a few tense moments. From the look on her face, I could tell that Grandma was feeling almost like a student waiting to get back her final exam.

Aunt Faith finished chewing and nodded slowly. "It's okay, Ruby," she pronounced. "Perhaps—a tups overdone. Maybe you should take it out five minutes earlier. I forgot to tell you that the timer is sometimes erratic. I more or less can judge it. But is all right." She smiled and patted Grandma Ruby's hand. I figured she had got a B, maybe a B+ for her test. I knew she was disappointed. Nothing less than an A would do for Ruby Fields.

Just then the nurse came over to tell us that we were too many visitors at once. Some of us would have to wait outside and take turns visiting. Lots of other patients had visitors too, and the ward did look pretty crowded.

Olivia and I were glad to escape. Miss Gertie had been there for some time, so she said good-bye too. So we left Grandma Ruby, Cousin Cecil, and Selvin with Aunt Faith. I was pretty sure they were going to be discussing Banana Bliss business.

Beware of Dog

Outside, Olivia began pacing. "Katani," she pleaded, "we have to sneak out tonight and get that necklace."

"Sneak out!" I shouted. "I can't sneak out. Grandma Ruby will kill me!"

"Shhh!" she warned me as she looked around. There were only a couple of boys kicking a soccer ball on the grass.

"Olivia, we're not in a spy movie." Although I *was*

beginning to wonder, what with lost necklaces, secret ingredients, and a suspicious man in a funny hat.

"Well, Miss America, you got a better idea?" I thought
that maybe I should talk to my grandma now, but I knew
Olivia would freak out if I suggested it. I didn't have another
idea, so I told her okay.

She looked at her watch. "Let's go back inside and get the
old people to leave." She whispered to me that she had made
a plan. "Listen . . . when the others go to bed, we'll slip out
and go to Ol' Madda Bird's house and get the necklace."

"What about the dog?" I asked.

She shrugged. "I have a plan for him, too," she said.

I didn't like the sound of that at all. I hated situations
like this. I didn't even like to watch them in the movies. I
was always the one screaming, "Don't go into the house," and
then I would keep my hands over my eyes until all the danger
was past.

Well, at least Olivia had a plan. I liked plans. I was known
as the organizational queen of the BSG back home. Plans
made me feel like everything was in control. But was everything really in control here?

We got back home by nightfall and ate some fried fish and
bammy, this flat cassava bread that everyone eats in Jamaica.
Where's the pizza? I wanted to ask. Then we cleaned up in the
kitchen and went to sit on the veranda, where Cousin Cecil
was getting ready to continue the River Mumma story.

When we got outside, Olivia was fidgety. She was
focused only on how to get back the necklace. But I was
secretly relieved. Not only did I want to hear the rest of the
story, but I was not excited about sneaking out to go wandering around in Jamaica at night. Olivia's plan was wigging
me out.

As soon as we were all settled and comfortable on the veranda, Cousin Cecil started. "Now where was I?"

"Orrin had found the River Mumma's comb and was planning to sell it," Selvin replied, before anybody else could. He was as eager as the rest of us to hear the end of the story.

11

"The River Mumma" Continued

Okay. Well, he wrapped the comb in some leaves from the bushes beside the river, put it in his pocket, and went home swinging his bucket of water with a very light heart.

Of course, he didn't tell his father about his find. Before he went to sleep, he unwrapped the comb and spent some time gloating over it. Then he wrapped it in an old handkerchief and put it under his pillow. It took him some time to fall asleep because he was so happy.

Twice during the night he had the very same dream. He was standing in the water and the River Mumma came up to him with a splash of her tail and called to him. She was very beautiful. He had thought that the "Mumma" in her name meant that she would be like an old witch.

She spoke in a gentle voice. "You can't keep my comb. I need it. Please leave it on the rock for me. Listen to what the stories tell you will happen if you don't give it back." Then she splashed away.

By morning, when he woke up, Orrin forgot about selling the comb to get money. All day he could think of nothing else but the beautiful mermaid. He went down to the river and spent some time hoping to see her, but she didn't appear. He couldn't wait for nightfall to see her once again. He was sure she would come to him in his dreams.

When she appeared in his dream that night, she seemed distressed. "You have to give me back my comb," she said, and she began to weep.

"No!" Orrin replied. "If I give you back your comb, I will never see you again."

The River Mumma shook her head. "No good will ever come from this. Put the comb back on the rock and forget about me."

"How can I forget you?" Orrin asked. "I've never seen anyone as beautiful as you. What's your name?"

The River Mumma smiled sadly. "Lake Water," she replied, and swam away. She didn't come back in his dreams like the night before.

What Orrin couldn't know was that the River Mumma had also fallen in love with him. Many times before she had shown herself, she had watched him as he'd come to fetch water. She knew he was sad, and longed to comfort him.

When she returned to her home in the depths of the river, she went to see the Old River Mumma, who was a thousand years old. "I warned you about visiting the mortals," she scolded Lake Water. "Now you have both fallen in love. What did you think could *happen? He must go his way, and you must go yours. If he doesn't return the comb, we will call for him in his dreams until he no longer loves you."*

"No!" cried Lake Water. "You can do something. I know you can do something so that we can be together. You can make it happen."

"Well," nodded the Old River Mumma, "if you are very sure, there might be a way."

"I'm sure! I'm sure!" cried Lake Water. "Even if he gives back the comb, I cannot forget him. I love him. I love him."

I could hardly believe this was Cousin Cecil telling the story. He was telling it with so much expression and passion, it pulled us all into the tale.

The next night, Orrin couldn't wait to go to sleep to dream about Lake Water. He felt so happy when she came in his dream. "Are you sure you love me?" she asked.

"Yes! Yes!" he cried.

"Will you do anything to be with me?"

"Yes. Yes. Anything."

"Very well. Bring the comb and come down to the river before daybreak. There is a way we can be together."

Orrin woke up a happy man. When he looked at the clock it was only three a.m. But he couldn't wait. He dressed carefully in his best clothes and put the comb in his pocket. He left his house and quietly walked along the path to the river. When he reached the river, everywhere was dark and creepy. What he could see of the river looked menacing. But he was not afraid. He couldn't wait to see his Lake Water and find out what she had planned for them.

As he waited, he began to fret. Suppose it was only a dream? Suppose she didn't come? His heart grew heavy. Time seemed to stand still. Then, just as the faintest glow began to lighten the sky in the east, he heard a splash in the water.

"Do you have the comb?" Lake Water asked.

He took it out of his pocket and showed her.

"Very well," she said. "Come into the water, and we will be united."

Without even a moment's hesitation, Orrin waded into the water. Deeper and deeper he went. Lake Water was beside him. He didn't know when he lost the comb. He didn't know when first his feet, then his body, began to change to water. He went side by side with Lake Water until the river closed over their heads.

He felt as if he was traveling in a deep cavern for a long time, and then, suddenly, he was rising above ground again, united with Lake Water as a beautiful lake somewhere in the middle of the island.

Some people were standing on a hill overlooking the lake. "Look!" They stared in wonder. "Where did this lake come from overnight?" they asked. Nobody knew.

Suddenly, Cousin Cecil's voice changed, and he sounded more like a schoolteacher. "That's the Moneague Lake, in St. Ann's Parish, the source of which nobody can explain. It rises and disappears underground as it pleases. But if you are brave enough to stand on the banks on a night when it has risen, you will hear loud splashes and the voices of a young man and a woman laughing as they play together in that dark, mysterious water."

Cousin Cecil stopped speaking, and there was silence for a while. I was thinking that this would make a really good movie. I could see the river princess now, all sparkly and beautiful.

"Good one, Dad," Olivia complimented her father.

"You just made that up?" Selvin's voice sounded as if he couldn't quite believe it.

"Of course." Cousin Cecil gave a brief laugh.

"I don't like how it ended," Selvin pronounced.

"What did you expect to happen?" Cousin Cecil asked.

Olivia chimed in, "Well, she could have used her magic to give him some treasure and the Old River Mumma could have turned her into woman so they could live happily ever after." I kind of agreed with her. That would have been a better ending.

Grandma laughed. "You are all too locked into happily ever after endings. But who says they couldn't be happy as a lake giving pleasure to people, providing food and water for all the lovely citizens of Jamaica?"

"I am glad you appreciate the moral of my story, Ruby," Cousin Cecil said with a laugh.

Olivia and I shook our heads. Who could be happy being turned into water in a lake?

"Actually, many folktales are about the origins of things and places. This is as good a one as I have heard," Grandma Ruby complimented Cousin Cecil.

"Thank you, my dear Ruby. I feel as if I just got an A for Language Arts." The formerly grumpy Cousin Cecil laughed. "And now, bedtime! Ruby, you have an early start, and the children are both going to school." Was it my imagination, or was he beginning to sound a bit more friendly? "No staying up to chat, or anything else," he warned, eyeing us almost as if he knew that we were planning something.

I cringed. I wanted to support Olivia, but I was uncomfortable about the whole plan. I wished I could tell Grandma, but how? I was sure that if we 'fessed up, she'd help us without ratting on us, but Olivia just would not agree. As we left the veranda, she made me swear for the third time not to tell anyone. There was no way out.

Olivia went on into her bedroom while I stopped and said good night to Grandma Ruby. When I walked into the bedroom Olivia was sitting on her bed with her arms crossed, a scowl on her face. "What's wrong?" I asked.

"Look!" she exclaimed, pointing to the window. A light rain had started. "We can't go to Ol' Madda Bird's house now. We'll have to wait until tomorrow night," she pouted.

I felt like I had just received a "get out of jail free" card.

CHAPTER

12

Hitting the Books

In the morning, Olivia woke me up very early. "Selvin is coming for us at six thirty—you must get up," she urged as I rolled over. I couldn't even imagine anyone in Boston getting up at five o'clock for school. I felt like I was living in the olden days, but I didn't want to hurt Olivia's feelings and tell her I was too tired to go to school.

I yawned my way through getting dressed. Remembering Sunday morning, I asked Olivia if there was any special dress code for visitors. She, of course, was wearing her uniform.

"Jeans will be fine for you," she told me. "And wear your sneakers."

Olivia had already packed her costume in her bag—a girl after my own heart: organized and ready to go. Since we hadn't been able to go looking for the necklace the night before, I had the time to use a little Kgirl magic (and a needle and thread) on Olivia's green blouse to make all the changes she wanted. It came out looking fab, if I do say so myself.

"Your grandma already gone to Bliss Bakery," Enid

informed me when I came into the kitchen. Enid had prepared heaping bowls of porridge made from green bananas for breakfast. It seemed that the banana—ripe and green—could be used to make all sorts of dishes. I was hungry, so I had some of the porridge, which was filling. But oh, for a bowl of cool, crunchy Oatios!

Olivia breezed through the porridge and followed it with two slices of bread and butter. She ate like Avery, the most athletic of the BSG, piling it on and enjoying every mouthful. When we were leaving, Olivia reminded Enid that she had promised to check on the goats for her, especially the young kids. I heard Enid grumbling softly, but she promised. Enid was like me: She wasn't a big fan of goats, especially Spotty.

On the way to school Olivia told me that her school was named the North Coast High School. She went on to explain that the high schools in Jamaica go from grades seven to eleven, and an additional two years in something they call sixth form, or "pre-college," in some schools. Olivia was in grade 7B. "You will see, Katani, that it is the best grade in the whole school." She laughed and tugged my braid.

"How many kids are in your class?" I asked as we made our way through the playground.

"Forty," she replied, like forty kids in a class was nothing.

"Forty kids," I gasped. "How does one teacher keep everyone under control?"

Olivia turned very serious. "Wait until you meet my teacher—she's totally in charge. No one would dare misbehave."

Kids were streaming into the school, a two-story building with an open quadrangle and an inner space planted with blooming shrubs. Concrete slabs formed the walkways between the plants, connecting one building to the next.

"Different grades take turns being responsible for this space," Olivia told me. "Everybody is really proud of it." I could see why. The garden looked like a professional gardener had designed it. I wondered if any students at Abigail Adams would be willing to plant and maintain a garden at our school. It seemed like kind of a cool thing to do.

I noticed a buzzing sound coming from all the rooms as Olivia walked me to her classroom. "All the classes are doing their Black History Month presentations today," she told me. In every room, students were busy rehearsing their parts and checking their costumes. With so many of them talking at once, I could hardly follow what they were saying, because most of them were speaking patois.

Olivia brought me into her classroom and introduced me to her homeroom teacher. "Miss Barnett, this is my cousin Katani, who has come from Boston with her grandmother to help out my aunt Faith with the bakery. She has never been to Jamaica before."

Some of the kids in the back of the class snickered. I turned and gave them my special Kgirl look—the one that let them know I was in charge. As the new girl for the day, I had to show them that I wasn't nervous. I really hoped they believed my *this is no big deal* performance, but I could feel my knees beginning to shake. *I should have stayed under those covers!* Then, I looked around the room, and one of the boys gave me a friendly nod. I relaxed a bit.

Charlotte's had tons of experience being the new kid, and she explained to me once how to handle it. You have to be nice but not too nice, or kids will think you are desperate for friends (which you are), which never works. And if someone talks to you, you have to respond or they will think you are a snob. So I gave the boy a friendly nod back.

Miss Barnett seemed to be a pleasant person. She was young, wore a light blue short-sleeved suit, and sported long extensions, which she tied at the back of her head. I couldn't help noticing how people dressed, fashion being my game and all. Comfort seemed to be the main Jamaican fashion statement, and I totally got that. It was so hot most of the time during the day, wearing heavy clothes would be silly. And there was no air conditioner. Instead, the classrooms were cooled by overhead fans.

As soon as I sat down I whipped out my Island Inspiration Notebook. I kept glancing up at Miss Barnett's outfit and the uniforms of all the students as I wrote.

7. Designing clothes for women in the tropics—think cotton, linen, and other cool fabrics that breathe. Comfort comes first!

8. Uniforms = no variation in how people dress. SO boring. I want to show off my fashion action—you know, start a craze! So hard to do when everyone has to wear the same thing.

Miss Barnett clapped once, and everyone sat down. I almost fell out of my chair when I heard how the students talked to the teacher. They were super polite, saying "Yes, Miss" and

"No, Miss" to everything, and there were NO wise comments coming from the back of the room—something that sometimes happened at my school. Everyone was quiet, sitting up straight and paying attention. The boys in my class at home would not believe it when I told them this story. I could hear Henry Yurt now: "Katani, you belong on the stage, girl."

Then it was time for the class presentation, a dramatization of parts of Marcus Garvey's life. First, a boy named Marius recited one of Garvey's speeches. Olivia and a group of students followed by singing "Amazing Grace." The performance was so good I felt like I was watching TV. Olivia's green blouse looked perfect for her role as Marcus Garvey's wife, and she remembered all of her lines.

"Very nice job, everyone," Miss Barnett declared when the presentation was over. Then she shocked me right out of my gold-trimmed sneakers with the silver shoelaces. "Katani, would you like to come up front and tell us about Black History Month in America?"

I looked at her, and she smiled to encourage me. Standing up in front of a class with kids you know is pretty serious, but standing up in front of kids you don't know is nightmare city. What was I going to say with no time to prepare? I walked slowly to the front of the room and turned around. The boy who had nodded earlier smiled at me. Suddenly, I felt okay. Maybe what I had to say would be of interest to the class.

"Well, as you know," I began slowly, trying desperately to think of something intelligent to say. "Black History Month is a celebration of the contributions African Americans have made to the development of the United States and the whole world. In America, people sometimes say we are a . . . a . . . ." I froze. What was that word people always use to describe America? With everybody staring at me, I couldn't concentrate! *Breathe, Kgirl,* I told myself. I took a deep gulp of air and went on, ". . . a 'melting pot' of a lot of different peoples from all over the world. African Americans are one of those groups, and during Black History Month we celebrate our culture with concerts, lectures, exhibitions, and . . . you know . . . that kind of stuff."

Okay, so far so good. But I was sort of out of things to say. The silence in the room was getting reeeeally long, so I just started blabbing the first thing I thought of.

"Maybe countries all over the world should also put aside a special month, or a week, or even a day, to learn the history of all the different peoples on our planet, as well. Because . . . um . . . the more we know about one another, the better we understand one another, and this can lead to a more tolerant and . . . uhhh . . . peaceful world," I ended. I thought I sounded kind of lame. I was really eager to sit down.

Miss Barnett seemed to understand that I was nervous. Everyone clapped politely, and she told me thanks on their behalf.

"What Katani has said is in keeping with Jamaica's own national motto: 'Out of many, one people," she said. "And she is right. The more we learn about one another; the more we understand one another; the more tolerant we become." When I returned to my seat, I figured that I had made a fool of myself. I buried my head in a book about Jamaican history, which turned out to be very interesting. I didn't even hear Olivia when she walked up to tell me it was time to go outside for recess.

"That was a good little speech," she said, obviously trying to make me feel better. "I can give you a tour of the school now, if you want."

"Sure," I agreed gratefully. I couldn't wait to escape from

her classroom, the scene of my completely embarrassing public-speaking moment.

We walked along the veranda that ran the length of the buildings, bumping into other kids as they chatted with their friends. The scene was just as crowded and crazy as the halls at AAJH.

At the end of one of the buildings, Olivia took me inside the school library, a large room filled with shelves of books. We walked over to a big history section with books about American history and Jamaican history and culture. "I wish I'd brought you here before the presentations today, Katani," she said thoughtfully.

"Yeah, maybe," I agreed. "Then I might have had something better to say!"

"My favorite is the fiction section, though," Olivia went on, guiding me over to another part of the big room. "Schoolbooks are kind of boring to me, but I love reading stories about people in other parts of the world."

"Have you read *Let the Circle Be Unbroken*?"

"No, I've never heard of it. Is it good?"

I couldn't believe it! Olivia had never even heard of one of my favorite books! "Yes, it's really good. It's all about these kids growing up in Mississippi during the Depression. I bet you have it here in the library. Let me look." I scanned the shelves until I found the "T" section for Mildred D. Taylor, the author. I couldn't believe it again. The book wasn't there.

"Too bad." Olivia sounded disappointed. "It seemed like a good story."

Suddenly I had one of those super-fabulous, brilliant ideas, a BSG change-the-world kind of thing, but I wanted to discuss it with Grandma Ruby and my friends at home before I even told Olivia. This library needed books. We could get

"Suddenly, I had one of those super-fabulous, brilliant ideas. . . ."

people to donate their favorite books and send them to Olivia's school. Maybe they could even send some of their favorites to us, too, like an international book exchange. I would send *Let the Circle Be Unbroken*, Charlotte would definitely send *Charlotte's Web* (her all-time favorite), Avery would probably send the bio of a sports star or something . . . I could totally see it all coming together in my head.

13

Ol' Madda Bird by Night

It's hard waiting for time to pass when you want to get something over with that you really don't want to do—like sneaking into a witch's yard in the middle of the night, for example. Dinner seemed to take forever that night. The adults were chattering away. They wanted to hear all about my experience at Olivia's school. Grandma Ruby, of course, was very interested. I wondered why they didn't notice how restless Olivia and I were. Finally, we announced that we were tired from the day's activities at school and we escaped as soon as we could.

We didn't change our clothes, but covered up with the sheets in case anyone looked in on us. When we heard Grandma coming, we pretended to be fast asleep. She stood at the doorway for a few minutes. I heard her say, "They must have had quite a day for themselves."

We had to wait until they were all settled for the night, and it was a good thing that we did, because Cousin Cecil, who had never checked on us since I was there, also came in. He opened the door and shone a flashlight around the room, then went over and closed the window, which Olivia had left open. It was as if he knew we were planning something and trying to prevent it. *Maybe I should just pretend to fall into a deep sleep*, I thought, *and Olivia will give up this crazy idea.*

But as soon as I heard Cousin Cecil go to his room and there were no more sounds of anyone moving around, Olivia whispered, "Dad never checks on me unless I'm sick. He works so hard during the day that he falls asleep as soon as his head hits the pillow. You think he suspects something?"

"He closed the window," I pointed out.

"I oiled the hinges this morning. It won't make any noise," she reassured me.

"Olivia, I'm worried about all this. I think we should just tell your dad. . . ."

"Katani." Olivia's voice sounded desperate. "I can't. I don't want to. . . . I can't disappoint him. I need to get that necklace back, and everything will be okay," she pleaded. "Let's go, now," she directed, and jumped out of bed.

I rubbed my eyes and sat up on the edge of the bed. How could I let Olivia down? She had been so nice to me and Grandma Ruby since we'd arrived. I had to help her now. After all, isn't that what family is all about?

There were no more sounds in the house. As silently as possible, we put on our sneakers and Olivia grabbed a large flashlight and a small bag. Despite her earlier assurance, the window seemed to creak loudly as she opened it. I shook my head. Not a good sign.

We waited a bit, but nobody stirred, so Olivia went through first. There was only a short drop to the ground. When it was my turn, I don't know what happened, but instead of landing on my feet, I fell over backward right onto my backbone and had to stifle the "ouch" that nearly escaped. Olivia gave a little nervous giggle. Again, we stayed frozen for a few minutes.

As we tiptoed away from the house, Olivia whispered, "Stay on the grass. The gravel makes noise." Maneuvering through the darkness undetected was so hard. I tried not to breathe.

We had to walk about a mile to the bakery, and after that, another quarter mile to reach Ol' Madda Bird's house along the winding country road. What if someone saw us? What would I tell Grandma Ruby? A pale fingernail moon gave us only a small fraction of light, but Olivia couldn't turn on the flashlight until we were well away from the house. The banana trees along the way seemed even more eerie than usual. There was no breeze, so they stood dark and still, looking like they didn't approve of what we were doing. I hugged myself, thinking, *Go home . . . go home . . .* I wondered if I could get Olivia to turn back.

Too late! The end of the driveway was in front of us. Then I heard a rustling sound. Before I could whisper, "What's that?" two shining orbs appeared. I ran for the bushes, and Olivia shone the light in that direction.

"Spotty!" Olivia exclaimed softly. "Come back, Katani." She spoke firmly to the goat. "How you get away? Go back to your pen!"

I don't know why—maybe he didn't like the way she spoke to him. Maybe he had never met any humans at night. Maybe he thought he was a watchdog—but whatever it was, he started pawing the ground, then lowered his head as if in anticipation of something to come.

"Run!" Olivia whispered. I didn't need to hear that twice. We ran down the rest of the driveway and onto the road, with Spotty charging behind us. When we reached the gate he simply stopped, turned around, and headed back to the house. Olivia started giggling. "That's one weird goat," she commented, shaking her head.

I didn't think it was funny, but we didn't have time to talk about Spotty the Psycho Goat. We set off, this time almost jogging. We really wanted to get this over with. Talk about dark and creepy! Once, we heard a car coming and hid in the bushes, with me praying there were no more Spottys around.

Finally we reached the bakery and crept past on the other side of the road, where the shadows hid us from view. There was a dim light coming from Selvin's house. As we turned onto the lane to Ol' Madda Bird's house, I had a sudden thought that made my belly flip-flop.

"What about her crazy old dog?" I asked Olivia.

"I'm ready for him," she replied, and took something out of the bag she was carrying. From the smell, I realized it was cooked meat. I heard the grin in her voice. That girl was a born spy. She thought of everything! Olivia was actually enjoying this, while I was feeling almost faint from anxiety!

We could barely see without the flashlight, but she didn't turn it on. We held hands and walked quickly. As bad as it felt to be doing this, there was something special about sharing this secret together. And then we were in front of Ol' Madda Bird's yard, which, like the others on the road, was in total darkness.

"Good! She's gone to bed," Olivia confirmed.

We cautiously lifted the latch on her gate. No sound from the dog. Phew. All of a sudden I breathed a huge sigh of relief. I hadn't even realized that I had been holding my breath. Quietly we crept up the little walkway, which was mostly grass. We reached the steps, and Olivia shone the light where we had last seen the necklace. It wasn't there! I looked at Olivia. "Okay, we're done here," I whispered. What would we do now?

But that girl Olivia went closer and shone the light over the veranda. We both froze when her light ran over Ol' Madda Bird, fast asleep in her chair, her head leaning to one side, her shades halfway off her face, and a piece of wood that she must have been carving lying on the floor beside her. I don't know why neither of us had thought earlier that since she was blind, Madda Bird didn't need to have a light on even if she hadn't gone to bed.

Her mangy dog was also asleep not far from her. My eyes bugged out of my head, and I grabbed Olivia's arm. The necklace was right beside him! Olivia stepped toward him carefully.

Creeeeeeeeak! Disaster! The dog opened one eye, then the other, and began to growl. Ol' Madda Bird sat up. "Who's it?" she asked loudly. I could hear that she was afraid. I suddenly felt sick to my stomach. What were we doing here? Olivia waved the meat around, then threw it to the other side of the veranda and whispered hoarsely, "Fetch." The dog got confused for a moment, then it went for the meat. Olivia ran up the steps, grabbed the necklace, raced back down, grabbed my hand, and whispered, "Run!"

As we sped away, I heard Ol' Madda Bird screeching, "Thief! Thief!"

"Dear God," I whispered a quick prayer, "please, help us out of this jam! I promise I'll never do anything bad again. I'll even be really, really nice to Patrice." Patrice was my bossy older sister, so that was a big promise. I kept repeating, "I'm sorry, I'm sorry," the whole time we ran. I couldn't even begin to imagine what Grandma would say about this if she ever found out.

Who's There?

When we reached the bakery, we paused to catch our breath. We had been running so fast I could barely speak. After our breathing quieted a bit, Olivia grabbed my arm and whispered, "Come on! We can't stop. We have to get away from here in case Ol' Madda Bird woke anyone up and they're looking for us!" I was sore from running, afraid that Ol' Madda Bird would somehow know it was us, and feeling really bad about scaring her. This wasn't an adventure anymore—now it was just trouble.

As we ran past the bakery we saw a wavering light coming from the back of the building. I heard Olivia gasp, then she pulled me deeper into the shadows. We stood quietly, hardly daring to breathe; whoever it was with the light would have to pass right by us. The light went out as the person came near. Just then a mosquito buzzed in my ear so loudly, I reacted without thinking by slapping at it.

"Who's there?" a woman's voice asked. Olivia stepped out into the road and shone the light on the person. "Precious!" she exclaimed. Then Olivia must have remembered how close we were to Selvin's house because she lowered her voice to ask, "What you doing here this time of night?"

"What *you* doing on the road, this time of night?" Precious hissed back at her. She was a sassy girl.

Olivia, of course, could not answer. They stood facing each other for a moment, then Precious said, "If you don't tell anybody you see me, I won't tell anybody I see you, 'cause I know you up to some badness."

With that, she stalked off. Olivia and I watched her

disappear into the darkness, but I thought I saw her climb into a blue SUV. We heard an engine start and the sound of a car driving away. That was weird. Was she meeting with Mr. Biggs again?

"That was a stupid thing to do, shining that light. What if it was a thief!" I yelled at Olivia.

"I wasn't thinking," she replied. "What we going to do now?"

"Olivia, I know that SUV," I told her. "I think it belongs to Mr. Biggs. I saw him sitting in it, talking to Precious, when we were walking back from church that day."

"You did? Why didn't you tell me?"

"You were so worried about the necklace, I totally forgot. But now I'm *sure* that Precious is a spy for Mr. Biggs! I mean, why else would she be sneaking around here with him at midnight? We have to go wake up Selvin and tell him right away."

"You mad!" exclaimed Olivia. "You forget why we are here?" She patted her pocket, where the necklace was safely stowed. "I just hope he didn't damage it. Let's just hurry home."

"But, Olivia—"

"Katani, if we tell Selvin, then he'll be asking why *we* are sneaking around here at midnight! Maybe it wasn't Mr. Biggs's SUV at all. It dark out here. Just forget about it."

We started off again, walking fast. I was still annoyed with Olivia, but now, with the mission accomplished, anger was beginning to give way to exhaustion and worry. I just knew there was something funny going on with Precious, and I was concerned about Ol' Madda Bird. I remembered something Grandma Ruby always said: *A lie is easy to tell and hard to manage.* I felt awful. What a huge mess!

"You think Ol' Madda Bird is going to tell anybody?" I asked.

"Doesn't matter," Olivia replied. "She can't know it's us."

"I thought you said she was a powerful witch," I answered sarcastically.

"But she's blind. She couldn't see us," Olivia answered nervously.

"She recognized you on the way to church," I reminded her. "Besides, she's really old and we may have scared her half to death. I feel terrible about that."

Olivia stifled a sob.

We didn't talk much after that. As we got closer to home I began to pray that Spotty was not waiting for us and that I wouldn't have to hear Olivia say "Run!" again that night.

Fortunately, Spotty wasn't around and we crept through the window and into bed. I was so tired that I didn't even lay out my clothes for the next day as I usually did. I could only put on my pj's and flop into bed. I wasn't quite sure what time of night it was, but the last time I had checked it was already past one o'clock.

After tossing and turning for a while, I tried to put my mind at ease so I could fall asleep. Maybe Olivia was right. Maybe that wasn't really Mr. Biggs's SUV. Anyway, there was no way we could tell anyone about it without getting ourselves in serious trouble. My last thought was that I was glad I wasn't going to school with Olivia that day and could run over and check on Ol' Madda Bird in the morning.

CHAPTER
14

Man-Eating Goats
and Inspiration

Bright sunlight filled the room when I woke up, which meant that Olivia had already left for school. *She must be so tired*, I thought sympathetically. Then I thought, *Serves her right for dragging us into this mess.*

I turned over, hoping that I could snooze for a little while longer. Crazy visions of flying wooden birds had kept me up all night, and I was sooo tired. All I wanted was sleep. Thankfully, there was a warm breeze wafting through the window, and I could hear the sounds of the laundry drying in the wind. It was like a TV commercial hypnotizing me back to sleep: "Relax, Katani. You're in Jamaica. *Go to sleep.* Last night was just a dream. Sleep . . . sleep . . ." My eyes closed to the happy images of dolphins leaping through the air in ballerina costumes.

Then suddenly I felt a slurpy tug at my shirt. Yuck! I rolled over toward the window and reached up to free my shirt. Groping around, my hand hit something soft and warm. And furry. My eyes flew open. Two big glassy eyes and a wet nose were looming over me. "Maaa!" it croaked.

I tried to leap out of bed to get away from this pj-eating-creature, but it had a hold of my shirt and wouldn't let go. I shook my shirt back and forth and grabbed my pillow and began beating the monster . . . the monster goat, that is. Spotty, forelegs on the window, his head actually inside the room, was making breakfast out of my pj top—my favorite pj top, in fact. He made a low growling sound again. "Ma-a-a-a." That was it!

I managed to yank my pj's from Spotty's mouth and ran screaming from the room straight for the kitchen, where I knew I would find Enid.

"Spotty was at the window trying to eat my pj's," I yelled as I burst in, only to come face-to-face with Grandma Ruby, who was sitting at the kitchen table, calmly reading a newspaper.

She looked at me over her glasses. "Good morning, Katani," she said with a smile.

"Grandma," I shouted. "That old goat wants to eat me alive." I couldn't believe that she was just sitting there so calmly after her precious granddaughter had been attacked by a man-eating goat.

"That Spotty too smart for a goat," Enid exclaimed. "Him get away again last night. You know," she continued, shaking her head, "one time that ol' goat up and go to church! We all sitting in the pews, just as quiet as can be, when all of a sudden we hear this scratchy sound at the back. Well, we turn around, and what do you know? Spotty come walking up the aisle like him was some kind of king! Him wearing Miss Mary's hat, too, that she lost in the wind the week before, just like it's a big, shiny crown. I never laugh so hard in my life!"

So that was the Spotty story that Olivia and Selvin were cracking up about! Enid chuckled and went on. "Yesterday

Mr. Selvin say him would tell Fitz to come for him and fix the pen. I gwan chase him away now." She reached for the bobo dread broom and took off like a ninja warrioress. I wouldn't want to be that Spotty right now.

"Good," I harrumphed. "At least someone knows how mean and nasty that goat is."

"Katani, sit down and have some Bliss. Goats don't eat people," Grandma said with a laugh.

Grumbling, I sat down and poured a glass of milk and helped myself to a giant slice of Banana Bliss. I took a big bite. It was a piece of pure banana happiness. At least my stomach was going to feel okay this morning.

"Him gone now!" Enid returned to the kitchen carrying the pile of clothes that Olivia and I had left all over the floor. They still had little bits of grass and stuff stuck to them from when we ran to get away from Ol' Madda Bird's house.

I saw Grandma Ruby glance over at the pile of grubby clothes in Enid's arms. I hoped she wouldn't think anything about it. No such luck. She stared at me over her reading glasses and said, "Katani, if you and Olivia are up to something, I suggest you tell me now. Olivia was so tired, she could barely stumble out the door this morning."

What could I say? I knew she was right. It was just that I was going to have to work up to spilling the beans. This wasn't like I had gone to the candy store without persmission or anything. This was the kind of thing parents grounded you forever for.

After a moment she said, "Well, just remember that what gone bad a mawning, cyan come good a evening."

I looked at her with a bewildered expression. The patois just didn't sound right coming from the mouth of the principal of Abigail Adams Junior High in Brookline, Massachusetts.

"I've been working with Miss Gloria in the bakery. She has a saying for every situation," Grandma explained, shrugging. "Get dressed now. After breakfast we're going with Selvin into Kingston."

"Why?" I asked without enthusiasm. I wanted to lounge around today and read in the hammock. Last night's crime caper had really zapped me into Silly Putty.

"Because, Missy" — Grandma pointed at me as she got up to wash her dishes— "Kingston is the capital city of Jamaica, and I am not going to miss seeing the sights. Besides, Selvin and I have a little business to do."

Suddenly the phone rang. Enid announced that it was Olivia, for me. I rushed to grab the phone from Enid's hands. I hoped Olivia had good news.

"Katani," Grandma Ruby yelled after me, "what's gotten into you?"

"Sorry, Enid," I mouthed as I pressed the phone to my ear. "Hello?" I said nervously, taking the phone into the next room. I definitely didn't want Grandma or Enid to overhear *this* conversation.

"I walked right by her house," Olivia said immediately, speaking quickly in a low voice. "She just carving away like nothing had happened. That old mangy dog growled at me, but I growled back. Him not know what to do. But, Katani, that Ol' Madda Bird yell out, 'Olivia, Olivia that you?' I didn't answer. I just kept walking. I think we're safe." Before I could say anything, she added, "I gotta go 'cause this is my friend's phone—see you this afternoon."

"Bye!" I blurted, right before she hung up.

I was so relieved, I did a little dance. Surely Ol' Madda Bird would have said something to Olivia if she'd recognized her from the night before. And she didn't seem to have been hurt or anything. Now I could breathe easy. Just maybe nobody would find out about Olivia's and my little adventure. But then I had another thought. I needed to tell Cousin Cecil and my grandma about Precious snooping around — but how could I without getting Olivia in trouble?

Road Trip

When Selvin heard about Spotty at the window, he laughed so hard, he had to pull the van over. "That's some goat," he said. "I told that Fitz to check the latch on his pen again. We can't figure out how that devil manages to get out. I think him need to go in the movies."

"I think him need to go to jail. Him one baaaad, evil goat." Both Selvin and Grandma howled at my attempt at patois. I was annoyed. I thought my accent sounded just like Enid's.

Selvin went on to tell us the latest local gossip. I sort of tuned him out since, after all, I didn't know any of the people he was talking about . . . until he mentioned something about "thieves trying to get into Ol' Madda Bird's house last night." I spilled some of my orange juice on my jersey before I could control myself.

"That's just terrible," said Grandma Ruby. "Now who would do such a thing?"

I had to fight hard to remain calm while Selvin told the story, which, he said, was all the talk in the village.

Suddenly I started worrying again. What if Precious let it slip she'd seen Olivia and me? We really weren't safe at all. Fortunately, Grandma Ruby was so interested in what he was saying that I don't think either of them noticed that my left leg was shaking so much I had to hold it down.

"First we deliver to a new client on the coast," Selvin

said, when he had finished the tale of Ol' Madda Bird's night-thieves. "Then we turn inland and travel over the mountain to Kingston."

We had barely turned onto the main coast road when a Mr. Biggs Better Banana Bread van passed us.

"Follow that van!" Grandma cried so loudly that Selvin stepped on the brakes and threw us against each other before he realized what she had said.

"Man, Aunt Ruby. You nearly mek me crash!" he shouted as he started up again. It was the first time I had ever seen Selvin flustered.

"So sorry,"' Grandma said, "but that man better not be going where we're going." I wondered what had got into her. The Grandma Ruby I knew definitely didn't go around shouting lines that sounded like they came right from spy movies.

Selvin tried to speed up, but our van wasn't very new and when we came to a section where they were working on the road, we were stopped to allow the oncoming lane of vehicles to pass.

"Oh, no!" I wailed, watching the big yellow van getting smaller and smaller. "They're getting away!"

By the time we started off again, it was impossible to catch Mr. Biggs's van.

"Sorry," said Selvin. "They gone. Why you want to follow them?"

"Selvin. Something is very wrong here. Everytime we go to deliver Bliss, Mr. Biggs is there before us. He seems to know everything we are doing. Perhaps it's time we had a little talk with Mr. Biggs."

Selvin shook his head and said quietly, "Ruby, you sure are something."

I sunk down in my seat. Now was the time to tell them

about Precious sneaking around the bakery in the middle of the night. But I just couldn't bring myself to do it. If I told about Precious, she'd tell about Olivia and me for sure. I didn't want to get Olivia in trouble . . . and, okay, I was afraid of how disappointed my grandma would be with me. Olivia had tied me to a promise I couldn't break, and I understood why, but it could be important to tell Grandma and Selvin what we had seen. I knew that Grandma would be terribly upset if Precious really was spying for Mr. Biggs and I knew about it and never told her! "BSG, where are you?" I whispered to myself. "I'm in trouble."

"What did you say, Katani?" Grandma turned around.

" I . . . I was just wishing the BSG were here. They would love to see all of this." That, at least, was not a lie.

"What's a BSG?" asked Selvin.

"Katani's best friends at home. Lovely girls, all of them," explained Grandma.

I sat back in my seat and imagined a big bash with Charlotte, Avery, Isabel, and Maeve on Negril Beach, a seven-mile-long beach with the whitest Jamaican sand you ever saw. I thought I might invite Nick Montoya (the nicest boy at my school) and Dillon Johnson (the freshest boy, as Grandma Ruby would say) and, of course, the twin Trentini goofballs. If I was in a good mood, I would even invite Henry Yurt, aka the Yurtmeister, president of our class and the biggest clown you ever met. But only if he didn't tease me about being so tall. I pushed away all my nerves about last night and consoled myself with visions of *Beach Party BSG*.

The road was very curvy, and driving on it made me sleepy. Next thing I knew, Grandma was poking me to wake up and look at the spectacular sights, like the winding riverbed with a ribbon of water flowing through far below the road, moss-covered hills, and bamboo groves. Who knew that Jamaica had bamboo?

"Are you feeling sick, Katani?" she asked with that suspicious look on her face again. "Why are you so sleepy?" I tried to keep my eyes open after that.

Eventually we came off a steep hill and entered Kingston. We drove down a long road past Jamaica House, which kind of looked like the White House in Washington, D.C. I took a picture for my friend Avery. She loved government stuff.

Finally, we stopped at a huge, old mansion called Devon House. Selvin said they had ice cream—famous ice cream. My eyes lit up. Yum! Chocolate Crunch was my favorite in the world. This whole mess with Olivia, Ol' Madda Bird, and Precious would have to wait.

Devon House was ginormous and old. But every room was filled with antique furniture and lovely decorations. All of a sudden, a beautiful girl walked by wearing a tropical skirt, a white tank top, and these stylin' silvery wedge sandals. My *Project Runway* mind started racing. I thought how cool it would be to have models dressed in the Kgirl Jamaica-inspired fashion collection parading around Devon House for a fashion show. I pulled out my Island Inspiration Notebook and started sketching right away.

9. *LOVING* antique details—lace, velvet, etc. Mix with tropical prints for beachwear? Could get *WILD*—in a good way!

"Katani, no school now. You are in Jamaica," Selvin called from the doorway.

I sighed and put my notebook away with reluctance. I could have stayed in that room all day thinking about summer dresses and pareos. That's what they call those long skirts you wrap around yourself when you're on the beach.

"Come on, girl. Ice cream a-waiting," Selvin called again.

I followed him outside. The tropical garden was covered with palms trees and these humongous large flowering shade trees. I wished the BSG were here right now. This place was perfect for a picnic.

Selvin steered me over to the Devon House Ice Cream Shop. What a variety of flavors with crazy-sounding names! No Chocolate Crunch, but I liked the guava jam I tried back at the house, so I figured I'd give the guava-flavored ice cream a go. Selvin recommended that Grandma Ruby try the Devon stout flavor. Stout is like beer. Whoa! Beer-flavored ice cream. Now that is definitely something you won't find back at home. I asked Grandma for a taste, but she refused and told me to behave myself. I couldn't wait until I told all the boys in my class about all of this. Riding horses on the beach, swimming with dolphins, man-eating goats, beer ice cream, turquoise water. Maybe we could set up a class trip to Jamaica!

We sat on a concrete bench under one of the shade trees nearby. After Grandma took the first taste of her ice cream, she sighed with happiness and joked, "Remind me about cholesterol when we get back to Brookline. This ice cream is the best I've ever tasted!" No doubt about it, Grandma Ruby had fallen head over heels in love with Jamaica.

Afterward we went to look in the stores. I love hotel and museum gift shops. They always have cool treasures that regular stores don't, and this one was no exception. We bought Jamaica T-shirts for all the family back home. A skirt made from crinkled material, colored yellow shading into green, caught my eye. I thought it would go perfectly with my black blouse—the Jamaican colors.

"You like that skirt, Katani?" Grandma Ruby asked, coming over to me and fingering the crinkly fabric. "I think we can get this for you. And how about one for Olivia, too? You girls deserve something nice. I'm so proud of the way you're trying new things and really connecting with our family here." She opened her arms and gave me a big hug.

Ugh. What a way to make me feel even more guilty! Now I really felt like a rat and a half for not telling her anything about the night before. That's the thing with doing something you know is wrong: It just eats at you and ruins your good times afterward.

I ended up buying five Rasta tams (a hat that looks a little like a beret) with fake dreadlocks attached at back. If I hadn't been feeling so guilty, I would have laughed out loud when I imagined the stir the BSG would cause when we all wore them at the same time.

As we were checking out with the T-shirts, skirts for me and Olivia, and tams for the BSG, I noticed all the books about Jamaica lined up near the register. I remembered that I hadn't told Grandma Ruby my idea about the book exchange with Olivia's school yet.

"Grandma, I have a great idea," I told her. After I explained it, a big smile spread across her face. "Why, Katani, I am so proud of you. That is a lovely idea."

Outside, I noticed that there was an Internet café near the mansion. I asked Grandma's permission to use it to send an e-mail to my friends back home. Grandma looked at her watch and said, "Make it quick, Katani. The Devon House chef will be coming out soon and I don't want you to have to search for us." She gave me some money, and I raced to the computer.

```
To: Isabel, Maeve, Charlotte, Avery
From: Katani
Subject: a NEW problem!

Hi, guys,

Am in Kingston, Jamaica's capital. Wait
until u see what I bought u in the
craft shop here. Just had some truly
scrumptious ice cream—guava flavor!
Olivia and me solved the problem I told
u about—really scary adventure—but now
I think we might have created another
one. Wish you guys were here to help!
Oh, and start thinking about collecting
your favorite books for a school library
here. More later.

—Kgirl
```

I hoped sharing books with a Jamaican school would make up for keeping the truth from my grandma and frightening Ol' Madda Bird. I wished I had the time to tell the BSG about this whole big mess; I could really use their help.

CHAPTER

15

Busted!

When I got back to where Grandma and Selvin were waiting, they were sipping iced tea and mopping their brows. The temperature was in the nineties and there wasn't a cloud in the sky, so it was really hot. I begged for a sip of Grandma's drink because I was thirsty too. *It's incredible how good a cold drink tastes in the sunny Caribbean*, I thought as the iced tea chilled me out.

I was in the middle of another slurp when a man in a crazy white hat came out. "Won't you come into the kitchen?" he invited us. Selvin had brought samples of Nana's Banana Bliss for the chef to taste. My grandma was so excited to present Nana's Bliss that her hands shook and she grabbed mine.

The kitchen in Devon House was jaw-dropping-amazing. I was going to have to describe this place to Avery's brother Scott and Isabel's sister Elena Maria—they both love to cook. The whole staff was dressed in white with these cool chef hats. They were cutting and chopping, and I even saw a whole fish head with the eyes and everything.

But the coolest thing, or should I say person, was the

head chef. I expected one of those chefs from TV—you know, like one of those smart-aleck types waving his hands around and telling everyone what to do. Except the chef wasn't a man after all. Instead, it was a small, soft-spoken woman named Chloe. She had come all the way from England and, before that, a country in Africa called Ghana.

"Welcome to my kitchen. Please be seated and I will be with you in a moment. I must prepare the crème brûlée for the Trinidad ambassador. I am sure you understand that the crème cannot wait," she explained as she smiled to us all. I stared at my grandma. I mean, who talks like that?

She sprinkled some brown sugar on a dish of custard, and then she grabbed this crazy blowtorch-looking thing and lit the dessert on fire! Flames shot up from the dish. I figured this must be some important ambassador to get such a fancy dessert. "She is caramelizing the sugar," Grandma Ruby explained.

After she washed her hands, Chloe came over and sat down at the table with us. I noticed that she was wearing this awesomely cool African bracelet—the bead design really popped. When I told her how much I liked it, she pulled it off her wrist. "Please," she said, "try it on." That lady did not have to ask me twice.

"I love this. It's so beautiful," I *oohed* and *aahed*.

"You may keep it," Chloe said casually, like it was noth-ing to give some girl you barely knew a beautiful bracelet. I looked at my grandma, who understood my dilemma. She tried to explain why I couldn't accept the gift.

"Chloe, this is so lovely of you, but I can't allow Katani to accept such a special gift." My brain was screaming, *Yes, you can*, but I didn't say a word. This situation was way too complicated for me to handle.

"Oh, but you must let her have it." Chloe looked at

Grandma Ruby. "This is one of my Jamaica bracelets. It symbolizes the motto of this beautiful nation." *Out of many, one people*, I remembered. "I make these bracelets for a hobby and give them away to people I like." She chuckled and gave me a wink. "I cannot be in the kitchen all the time. The beads relax me. I would like Katani to have this bracelet as a remembrance of her trip to Jamaica, so that she can share her good times and memories with those around her."

This time, Grandma nodded okay. I jumped out of my seat and gave Chloe the biggest hug. I practically lifted her off her feet.

"I'm going to make some notes and sketch the patterns on these beads in my design ideas notebook right away!" I told her, pulling out my Island Inspiration pad.

10. *Beaded Jamaican bracelet from Chef Chloe—beads are African-inspired and* GORGEOUS. *Research connection between African and Jamaican art?*

"Katani is an aspiring fashion designer," Grandma Ruby explained as I scribbled.

"That is wonderful, Katani!" Chloe said with a smile. "If you like my bracelet, you must have good taste," she joked. Then she turned back to business. "Now we must try the Bliss."

Chloe nodded to Selvin, who was falling all over himself to impress her. He had laid out perfectly cut slices of Bliss. All of us were nervous as Chloe lifted a slice to her mouth and took a tiny bite. I guessed chefs had to take small bites. I mean, if they took big bites day after day, they would get really huge.

I was surprised when Chloe took another bite and then another. Finally a big smile spread across her face. "This is perfectly wonderful banana bread. I think we would love to serve it to our customers." And then she squished her eyebrows together. "But unfortunately, we won't be able to start serving your marvelous Bliss for at least two months."

"But, Chloe, why? We can deliver tomorrow, if you like," Grandma Ruby asked in a worried voice as she leaned forward in her chair.

"Yes, Madame, and I am sorry," she said in a very soft voice. These Jamaican people were so polite. "But, we have just this very morning signed a contract for two months with the Manteca Bay Bakery Company for their Banana Bread."

Grandma looked at Selvin, who straightened his shoulders and stood up. I felt like crawling through a crack in the floor.

"We thank you for your time, Chloe. I hope that you will allow Nana's Banana Bliss to come back and present to you again." Grandma offered her hand to Chloe

I wondered if I should even give my bracelet back, but I could see that Chloe looked very upset too.

"Yes, yes, definitely. You must set up an appointment with my assistant. I am sure that we can work something out at the end of the contract with Manteca. It will be fine, you will see." What a terrible situation! I didn't know who I felt worse for: Grandma Ruby or Chloe.

Selvin packed up the rest of the Bliss and with that, we left the fancy kitchen and made our way in silence to the car. How disappointing.

Once we headed down the road, Grandma turned to

Selvin and said, "I told you that man must be spying on us. How would he know that we were coming here?" I could have sworn sparks were flying out of her eyes.

"Come now, Ruby," Selvin tried to explain. "Him go all over the island. I think it's only a coincidence." Grandma snorted in disbelief and turned on the radio to the local reggae station. I couldn't help thinking about Precious. Grandma might be right about Mr. Biggs spying on us, and I was pretty sure who had betrayed Nana's Banana Bliss. But how could I tell her?

I don't remember much of the trip back home after that. I was so tired that I fell into one of those sleeps that you don't even know you are asleep until someone tries to wake you up. Then you feel like you are flying in from another planet. I didn't open my eyes until we drove into the driveway and I heard the goats.

I raced out of the van, mumbling that I needed to take a shower. Olivia was in the bedroom asleep. I shook her awake. "Olivia, Olivia, we are in deep trouble. Wake up now."

"Katani, I can't, I'm too tired," she groaned, and then put the pillow over her head. But I wasn't having any of it. I ran to the bathroom and wet a face cloth with cold water. I ripped the pillow off her head and placed the cold cloth on her face—an old trick of my sister Patrice's when she wanted me to get up on Saturday mornings.

Wouldn't you know it? It worked for Olivia, too. She was awake in a flash. "Katani, what is your problem?"

"Olivia, it's time to tell the truth." I lost no time telling her what Grandma Ruby had said about Mr. Biggs spying. She finally got it. She looked at me with those big brown eyes of hers. "Do you really think that Mr. Biggs and Precious could be trying to sabotage the bakery?" she asked.

"I don't know what this is all about, Olivia. But we've let it go too far. We have to tell." I twirled my hair around my finger.

"What he could do, Mr. Biggs?" she asked in a dismissive tone.

"I don't know, but if he wants Banana Bliss, he could be planning to get to every resort before we do. And Precious could even give him Aunt Faith's secret recipe"

"You're right, Katani. But, I'm going to be in big trouble." She shook her head.

"You aren't the only one, Olivia. My grandma is going to be pretty unhappy too."

Suddenly we heard Cousin Cecil's truck come into the yard and park. Both of us flinched when we heard how hard he slammed the door.

"What's my dad doing home so early?" Olivia asked, sounding anxious. "It's only four o'clock."

I didn't know, but immediately I began to feel apprehensive. Olivia and I grabbed each other's hands. There was trouble ahead.

Then we heard Grandma calling, "Olivia, Katani, please come here immediately."

It was an order, not a request. Hand in hand, we dragged ourselves to the veranda, where Cousin Cecil, Selvin, and Grandma were standing, waiting . . . for us. I knew that our faces said that we were guilty even before we were accused.

"Tell us, Katani. Tell me, Olivia," Cousin Cecil said. "Where were you last night when we thought you were both in bed asleep?"

I couldn't even manage to stammer out an answer. Olivia and I looked at each other miserably. Had Precious ratted on us to Cousin Cecil?

"This morning, first thing, everybody at the bakery was talking about how thieves tried to break in on the old lady you children call Ol' Madda Bird, who is not a witch, as you ridiculous children believe. It is unthinkable that anybody around here would try something like that, so a couple of us went to investigate. We found out that late last night someone saw Precious on the road near Ol' Madda Bird's house and the bakery."

"I know what she was doing!" I blurted out. I couldn't believe I was interrupting Cousin Cecil when he already looked so angry that fire could shoot from his eyes any minute. But for the sake of Nana's Banana Bliss, I just had to tell him what I knew. "Precious is—

"Katani, this is not the time," Grandma Ruby scolded me.

"But, Aunt Ruby, Dad, you don't understand," Olivia defended me. "Precious is—"

"Enough!" Cousin Cecil thundered. Olivia and I were shocked into silence. Cousin Cecil was stern sometimes, but I had never heard him raise his voice . . . until now. "It is no matter for you girls what Precious is or isn't. As a matter of fact, I've just come from her house, and she has explained everything."

"So you know why she was there last night?" I asked.

"Yes, Katani, I do, although I certainly do not feel the need to discuss employee issues with you girls. Ruby, you and I can have a talk about it after we are finished here."

Grandma Ruby nodded. I guess if Cousin Cecil knew what Precious was up to, then everything was okay for Banana Bliss. But everything was definitely not okay for Olivia and me.

"Let's get back to Ol' Madda Bird," Cousin Cecil

continued. "That poor, old, blind woman was so frightened by the intruders, she yelled for help, but when her neighbors came, they saw no one, only the open gate. The dog must have frightened them away. She is sure there was more than one."

I knew then that, as my mother would say, our goose was really cooked. It wouldn't be possible even to try to make up an excuse. If only Olivia had listened to me, I thought; then immediately felt guilty. I could have refused to go. Perhaps she would not have gone alone. My thoughts were all confused. I suddenly felt like lying down . . . on a nice beach somewhere, anywhere, as long as it was far away from here.

"Fast-forward," Cousin Cecil continued, "to Precious leaving the bakery and meeting Olivia and Katani, who couldn't say what they were doing on the road that time of night. It didn't take long to figure out that our two young ladies here were on a midnight mission to scare a poor old lady who has done no harm to anyone."

Grandma Ruby put her hand to her chest. "Katani, is this true?" I have never seen such disappointment in my grandmother's eyes. Would Grandma Ruby ever forgive me?

"Do you want to tell us why you went to terrorize that poor woman?" Cousin Cecil demanded, after a silence.

Olivia gulped several times. Everybody was staring at us. I couldn't speak. I tried to open my mouth, but nothing came out. I looked at Olivia and put my hands up. I was hoping she could pull it together. I couldn't look at Grandma, so I just hung my head.

"Well?" Cousin Cecil said impatiently.

Finally, with many stops and starts, Olivia told them the whole story, in the tiniest voice I had ever heard from her. I finally managed to squeak a few words out too. "We never expected her to be on the veranda; we just thought she would be asleep in her house, like everyone else."

"We would never have scared her on purpose. We only wanted to get back the necklace from the dog," a contrite Olivia explained.

"Well, I'm sure she's grateful for that," Grandma Ruby said sarcastically.

Ouch. I was feeling terrible. What had I been thinking? A quick thought from health class raced through my mind: *The teenage brain sometimes prevents adolescents from predicting the consequences of their actions.* Perhaps I could plead adolescent confusion or something. I glanced over at Grandma Ruby. My defense died quickly when I saw her expression. It was her after-school Detention City look!

"Why didn't you tell me you wanted to wear the necklace?" Cousin Cecil asked. Somehow his voice no longer sounded so stern.

"You won't let me wear Mom's jewelry," Olivia insisted. "You say I'm too young, but I think it's because you don't want anybody wearing her things—not even me."

Cousin Cecil stared at her. Then he said, "Is that what you think, Liv?"

Olivia burst into tears, and he bent down and hugged her. I could see the surprise in Selvin's face.

"It's true, I don't think you are old enough to wear her jewelry. Some of the pieces are very expensive and a bit too sophisticated for you just yet. But, if you had told me you wanted to wear that necklace to church, I would have allowed you."

Olivia sobbed even louder. Later she told me that only her mom had ever shortened her name to Liv, and when her father called her that, she felt as if her heart were breaking.

But I was in trouble too. "I'm very disappointed in you, Katani," Grandma Ruby began. "If you had told me about all this, we could have solved the problem without terrorizing the old lady and putting yourselves in danger. What *were* you thinking? Wandering on the lonely country road at night? Suppose something had happened to you? What would I tell your parents?"

I couldn't say anything. Mixed emotions raced through me. Anger with Olivia, shame because I had let Grandma down, but also a feeling of being terribly misunderstood. Didn't Grandma know about loyalty to friends?

"You are going to be grounded for the rest of this trip," she added.

I wanted to cry as well. Here I was in Jamaica, and now I was going to be grounded. It wasn't even my fault. I just shook my head back and forth. I wasn't the criminal here. I just wanted to help my cousin. The tears were dripping down my face.

"No!" Olivia cried. "It's my fault. Please don't punish Katani. I made her do it." I was grateful to hear her say that, and I reached over and squeezed her hand.

"Ruby," Cousin Cecil said. "Can I see you inside for a moment?" They both went into the living room while Olivia and I tried to dry our tears. But Olivia was so upset, she threw her arms around me and kept saying how sorry she was. I just hugged her tight. I knew in my heart that it wasn't all her fault. We had both got carried away by that lost necklace.

Enid stood at the kitchen door, shaking her head. "Pickney!" I heard her say. "Always getting into trouble."

Selvin said, "I'm not sorry for you nutty girls. Why didn't you come to me? I could easily have gotten back the necklace.

16

Party On

By the time Grandma and Cousin Cecil had returned from their *What are we going to do with these girls?* conference, Olivia and I had calmed ourselves down and were preparing to take our medicine. I knew I had messed up really big-time, and I fully expected to be spending the rest of my vacation in Jamaica in Olivia's bedroom. I just hoped Grandma Ruby would let me read, even if it was books on how to be a really good person or how not to lose your privileges forever. That would be a better fate than staring out the window at Spotty and counting split ends.

Cousin Cecil spoke first. "We have decided on the consequences for your actions. We don't want that poor old lady to spend another night worrying, so I am going over there now to explain what happened. Tomorrow, you two young ladies will pay Miss Eva a visit."

"Miss Eva?" Olivia and I said in unison.

"Yes," Grandma Ruby said in a voice I hadn't heard before. "Madda Bird has a name, just like everyone else. Her mother named her Eva."

Olivia and I both looked down at the ground and then quietly slunk off to our bedroom as Grandma Ruby picked up her book and headed for the veranda. I wondered if this meant Grandma had decided not to ground me after all.

When Olivia and I got to the room, we flopped down on the bed with simultaneous groans. Olivia turned to me with such a miserable expression on her face that I had to stifle a huge giggle.

"Katani, I just can't go over to Ol' Madda Bir—I mean, Miss Eva's, empty handed. I just can't."

"I know what you mean, Olivia." I responded and turned over to look at her. "It would be so totally cheesy to just show up and say, 'I'm sorry,' then stare at the ground like a pair of pathetic goofballs. But what can we do?"

And then it hit me. I jumped off the bed, kneeled down, and pulled out my suitcase from under the bed. I started tossing clothes everywhere. I was sure I had brought them . . . they were in here somewhere. I was sure of it.

"What are you looking for, girl?" Olivia kneeled down beside me.

"Ahh, here it is." I yanked out a bag with a pair of knitting needles and some leftover yarn I had from a project back home. "I always travel with them. You never know when you might have some downtime and want to make something or just want to chill out. Knitting is great for that," I told her.

I pulled out the two balls of yarn I had brought with me, one small white and one larger pink. If I worked diligently I could have the scarf by midnight. I was psyched! I had my mission.

"Oh, that is so pretty. I love that color. It's like a rose," Olivia said as she fingered the soft yarn. "What are you going to do with it?"

"Tonight I am going to sit in this room and make the prettiest scarf I can for Miss Eva. She can wear it if a wind comes up at night. With these needles, it'll knit up nice and lacy so she won't get too warm." I jumped up on the bed and began right away. Knit one, purl two. I could feel my mind focusing and relaxing at the same time—a design was forming in my mind—something perfect for the old woman who obviously loved birds.

"Well, I like your idea, Katani, but what am I going to do? I can't knit." Olivia sighed.

We sat in silence for a minute when all of a sudden Olivia jumped off the bed and snapped her fingers. "I know—I know what I gwine do. What do you think of this, Katani. . . ."

The Party Planners

Olivia and I worked all evening while Grandma and Cousin Cecil sat on the veranda chatting and listening to music as if nothing had ever happened. I kept waiting for one of them to come in the room and ask us what we were planning, but they never did. Cousin Cecil never went into the kitchen at all. Both of them just let Olivia and me do our thing. Olivia wouldn't even let me in the kitchen to see what she was doing.

I worked all night on the scarf and I was very happy with the design. When I set aside my needles I realized that it was dark outside and everyone was asleep. I was starving. I snuck quietly out of the room on my tiptoes. I certainly didn't want to wake anyone tonight, but I needed a glass of milk or something. I crept through the main room, past Grandma Ruby's bedroom, and into the kitchen.

When I turned on the light and saw what Olivia had created, I almost couldn't believe my eyes. Suddenly, I heard footsteps. I spun around. Grandma Ruby was standing in the doorway. I looked at her, and she held out her arms. I flung myself across that room so fast, I could have qualified for the Olympics. I laid my head on my grandma's shoulder and let out the longest breath of my life. It was like I had been holding it all night long. She patted my back, and suddenly I knew that all was forgiven.

We sat down at the table and both had a glass of milk and a bit of Banana Bliss.

"Katani dear, sometimes it is difficult to decide between loyalty and stepping up to the plate when the truth is needed—it's even difficult for grown-ups. You will face many decisions like this on your journey to adulthood. I hope you will think carefully about each decision that you make." That's all my grandma was ever to say to me about Olivia's and my nighttime adventure. But it was all she needed to say.

The next morning, when I woke up, Olivia was already up and working in the kitchen. I threw on a sweatshirt and rushed to join her. We had both agreed that it would be proper to make breakfast for everyone. I looked around for Olivia's creation, but she must have put it away.

"Olivia," I asked, "do you want to tell them the plan, or do you want me to?"

She thought a moment. "I think you should do it. But I want you to . . ." She lowered her voice and explained the rest in a whisper.

When Cousin Cecil and Grandma and Selvin entered the kitchen, they could only stare at the table in surprise.

"Well, now, young ladies. What have we here?" Cousin Cecil asked.

Olivia and I had set the table like Martha Stewart. We had flowers and napkins folded like fans. We had grabbed some wildflowers and put them in a vase. Olivia, who turned out to be an awesome cook, had made eggs and bacon (at my request) and huge platefuls of traditional Jamaican food for everyone. There was Enid's run down, green banana porridge, fried dumplings, and ackee and saltfish. "You can't come to Jamaica and not eat our national dish," Olivia explained with a smile, pointing to a bowl full of stuff that looked like scrambled eggs with bits of brown stuff in it. "We take the ackee, which is this red fruit, and boil it and cook it in oil with shredded salted codfish and *plenty* of onions and pepper."

"Why, that sounds perfectly delicious, Olivia," Grandma commented.

"Please help yourself! I'll be right back," Olivia urged with a wink at me, and dashed out of the room.

As everyone sat down, I made the announcement we had planned out: "Olivia and I are very sorry for our mistake. To make up for it, we have worked on a surprise for Miss Eva. Olivia will go first."

Olivia walked back into the kitchen carrying the most beautiful cake, covered with coconut. It almost looked like a wedding cake, with three tiers. At the top, Olivia had fashioned a white bird made out of frosting.

Cousin Cecil looked at his daughter with such pride and began to clap. Olivia beamed.

When it was my turn, I unfolded the pink scarf. In the middle I had knitted a small white bird. Selvin whistled. "Very good work, Katani. You are a very good artist."

Grandma just smiled, but I knew she was proud too.

After breakfast, Olivia and I cleaned up. It was decided that we could go visit Miss Eva that afternoon. Grandma was off to the bakery, and Cousin Cecil was going to meet with some American grocery store representatives. Selvin

CHAPTER
17
Falling Over

As we went down the steps to the beach, we could see and hear the rushing water of the falls. "This view is amazing!" I shouted over the whoosh of the water. The falls were steep in places and scary looking in others, with lots of overhanging tree branches. But there were also a few calm pools where people were wading and splashing around. At the bottom of the path we found a beautiful stretch of light brown, powdery sand, with palm and almond trees gnarled and twisted by the wind, and clear blue waters stretching out into the distance. There were buoys marking the limit for swimming. The end of the falls roared into the sea.

"Want to climb?" Selvin asked.

I think my eyes bugged about a mile out of my head. "Climb up that waterfall? Are you crazy?" I asked him.

He just laughed. "Not crazy, Katani. People do it all the time. And I can be your guide. I have climbed these falls many times."

"Come on, Katani. Let's do it! Those girls look like they're having fun." Olivia pointed at some girls around our age, standing in a little pool about a quarter of the way up the falls, laughing and splashing. She had a point: They did look like they were having a blast. But feeling like the most un-athletic girl on the planet, I wasn't sure if I was up to scrambling over sharp, slippery rocks.

"There is a craft village at the top," Selvin said temptingly when he saw the hesitant look on my face. "Shopping, Katani. Clothes and beads and fabrics . . ."

Well, that settled it. I'd just have to push aside my fears and go for it. Sometimes fashion requires sacrifice.

Selvin, Olivia, and I linked hands and formed a human chain. As I stood at the foot of the falls, staring up at the tumbling, noisy, foaming water, my knees started shaking. I was holding Selvin's hand, but I remembered the saying that a chain is only as strong as its weakest link. I definitely didn't want to be that weak link. Olivia and Selvin were depending on me.

"Ready?" Selvin asked. I stood tall and gripped his hand a little tighter.

"Ready!" Olivia and I shouted back.

Climbing was seriously intense. We had to pick our way along paths where the water wasn't rushing down too strongly, choosing each step carefully. Once, I slipped and lost hold of Selvin's hand. He helped me to get up, and we continued climbing. "You can do it, Katani!" Olivia shouted in my ear. Sometimes we had to pull strongly to help one another over a tricky patch. I was sooo glad when we reached a calm area where we could rest in the pool of water there. What an adventure!

As Olivia and I flopped down into the cool water, I noticed that we had caught up with the girls we had seen climbing up ahead of us. They were lounging in the water nearby.

"Hi!" Olivia greeted them, like she had known them all

her life. I was so impressed by how that girl could talk to any-one. "That climbing was hard, wasn't it?"

"Definitely," a girl with a head full of tiny, beaded braids answered her. "I think we almost lost Megan a couple of times." She looked over at her friend, who was rubbing a scraped knee, and the three of them started laughing.

Megan shrugged as she giggled. "I'm pretty much terrible at athletic stuff. And our guide said it would be tricky."

"That's right, I warn you!" remarked the woman with them, laughing too. Her long braids were pulled up into a ponytail, and she wore a snug-fitting, neon green and bright yellow athletic shirt. It was totally sporty-chic.

I could tell right away from their accents that these girls weren't from Jamaica. They were from the States, like me. "Where are you from?" I asked.

"California," the girl with the beaded braids answered. "I'm Leesha, and this is Megan and Kayla. And our guide is Vicki."

"I'm Olivia!" my cousin introduced herself, jumping up and splashing through the shallow water to give high fives to all the girls and Vicki. I waved from where I was sitting. "That's my cousin Selvin, and this is Katani," she informed them. "She's a little shy, but I know you will like her." She smiled at me.

I just shook my head at her. That Olivia certainly had a way of making friends. "I'm bad at sports too," I said to Megan, and we smiled at each other.

"Hey, why don't you guys join up with us?" Kayla suggested. "We could be like one super-long human chain! Is that okay?" She turned to their guide.

"Okay by me," Vicki answered.

Selvin nodded. "Good idea."

We all linked arms again, Vicki first, then me and Megan, Olivia, Kayla, Leesha, and finally Selvin. With everybody pulling together, it was SO much easier to wiggle our way through the water. I was really happy to have another non-athlete there with me (and I think Megan was too), but at the same time, I was totally inspired by Vicki's awesome, sporty attitude—and awesome fashion choices. *Maybe sports and fashion can go together*, I thought as I helped Megan step over a huge, pointy rock.

At the top we all collapsed, giggling, in another pool of cool water. I was having so much fun talking to the girls that I didn't even notice that Selvin wasn't there until Olivia suddenly tugged on my shirt. "Do you see what I see?" she whispered, pointing behind me. We all turned around. There were Selvin and Vicki, browsing the shops in the craft village, grinning like crazy and standing *very* close together. Boy, that had happened fast!

"Oooo," Leesha said teasingly. "Vicki and Selvin, sittin' in a tree—"

"K-I-S-S-I-N-G!" Olivia finished. We all burst out laughing. Okay, so maybe it was a little fourth-grade, but I had to admit that Selvin and Vicki did make a very nice-looking couple.

On the way home, Olivia and I teased Selvin about showing his romantic side. "You gwine call your new girlfriend, Selvin? You better," Olivia laughed.

"Pickney," he grumbled, but I could see he was trying hard not to smile. "Empty barrel mek de most noise. By and by, yuh wi si."

"Um, translation?" I asked Olivia. "Did he just call us empty barrels?"

She laughed. "It means we don't know what we are talking about."

"We know more than you think, Mr. Selvin," I said, trying to sound very proper. "Olivia and I are *very* mature for our age."

Then I stuck my tongue out at him.

18

A Grand Apology

Walking over to Ol' Madda Bird's—oops—Miss Eva's house was positively one of the most embarrassing and funniest experiences of my entire life! Here's how it all went down.

At first it was just our family. Cousin Cecil walked next to Olivia, who was carrying her dreamy coconut cake (I couldn't wait to dig into a piece of that!) on a tray surrounded by napkins and plastic forks. Selvin was carrying a box full of cups for tea, and Grandma Ruby had a large bottle of lemonade. I was carrying my scarf, which I had wrapped in bright yellow tissue paper. On top I had glued a flower from the garden. I knew Miss Eva was blind, but who doesn't love to unwrap a present, even if you are really ancient and can't see? Plus, I thought the present would help with the lameness of the whole situation.

"Katani," Olivia whispered, "does making an apology make you feel like you about to eat a plate of glue?"

"Whoa, Olivia! Do I know what you are talking about, girlfriend. You know it's going to be really bad when you stumble about trying to figure out the right words but your tongue seems glued to the roof of your mouth, and in the end all you manage to spit out is a pathetic 'sorry.'" Olivia and I linked pinkies—the secret girlfriend code that meant *I'm on your team.*

At least our plan to make an apology party for Miss Eva made me feel like we were paying her back for our dumb mistake. Even if I had a glue attack while I was apologizing, I could still give her the present.

As we headed down the path, I could tell that Cousin Cecil was proud of Olivia for all her efforts. He kept looking over at her and smiling. His grouchy exterior seemed to melt away as we walked.

By the time our procession reached the bakery, there were about five people hanging around, looking as if they were waiting for our arrival. But how did they know we were coming?

Cousin Cecil looked at Selvin and shook his head. "The gossips have been beating the drums."

Grandma Ruby whispered in my ear. "Katani, keep your head high and don't let anything they say bother you." Grandma walked by and nodded to the nosy gaggle of ducks—that's what they all looked like to me. "Good afternoon, ladies, lovely day in Jamaica."

I had to give it to Grandma Ruby. She sounded like a queen. Cousin Cecil and Selvin looked at her with these big, wide grins. They were obviously impressed.

Apparently, the news that we were the culprits and were on our way to apologize to Miss Eva had spread, cell phone-fast. It was shocking how fast! "Nothing is private in Jamaica, Katani. You just have to ignore those gossiping girls," Olivia leaned in to tell me. "They just like to talk . . . and talk . . . and talk."

I giggled. "I know lots of people like that at home."

As we walked by the group of chattering ladies I heard one of them say, "There they are. Sneak out in the middle of the night and scare someone like that. What dem naughty girls think?" Everyone around was nodding as the big woman in the purple dress spoke. I figured she was the leader of the gossips.

I was totally embarrassed to have all these people staring at me, but at the same time I wanted to laugh. It was like I was in one of those bad reality TV shows. If only the BSG could see the Kgirl now—walking down the street on her way to apologize for the dumbest mistake of her whole life, followed by a group of people she didn't even know on the sunny vacation island of Jamaica. Was this really happening? Reality check!

By the time we started walking up the lane to Miss Eva's house, even more people had appeared. We were now like a parade. I almost expected someone to start selling balloons and peanuts. Grandma and Cousin Cecil were marching in front. Olivia and I had managed to fall in behind them—kind of like two prisoners. Then came Selvin, who seemed to be enjoying the growing crowd. I could hear their excited chatter and laughter. I honestly didn't know what all the gawkers expected would happen. Did they think I was going to fall down on my knees and weep and wail and beat my hands on the ground? I almost laughed out loud at the image of me acting like some fragile, tragic heroine from an old movie.

When one of the women following the party gave me a funny look, I really longed for one of those closed carriages from the olden days. Or even the baseball cap I had left on the bed in Olivia's room because I thought it would mess up my hair. *Pride, foolish pride*—I could hear my mother now.

My whole vision of a nice little private apology party with Miss Eva was fast disappearing. This was like an inquisition! I looked over at Olivia and Grandma Ruby. They were chatting up a storm, as if they were strolling to a garden party. But as I sidled up to Olivia, I heard her complaining to Grandma, "Mek dem so fass! Mek dem nuh leave us alone and gwan a dem yard go mind dem own business!" She had slipped into speaking pure patois, and I could hardly understand her.

"Olivia, what are you saying, girl?" I asked her.

She grabbed my arm and gave a huge smile. Then, through her gritted teeth she whispered to me, "I wish everyone would just mind their own business, don't you?"

I understood the game now. I smiled and nodded at everyone. "Yes, I do. I wish they would go home and watch *Oprah*," I told her out of the corner of my mouth.

"Good afternoon, Miss Seldon." Olivia nodded graciously at an old lady wearing a muumuu and carrying a giant white cat.

Just when I was about to hand my beautifully wrapped present to my grandma and tell her I was too tired to party, the apology parade reached Miss Eva's gate. It was too late to escape.

Cousin Cecil called out, "Afternoon, Miss Eva. It's Cousin Cecil Palmer and some other folks come to see you. Hold the dog."

I couldn't tell if Miss Eva was surprised or not. She turned her head, got up a bit shakily, felt along the veranda rail, and walked toward her little mangy dog, which was acting like he was some huge guard dog. He kind of reminded me a little of Marty (except Marty lacked the guard dog personality). Miss Eva held the little mutt by his collar, dragged him toward the door, nudged him inside, and closed the door behind him.

She might have been really old, but she seemed stronger than she looked. We could hear the dog barking and trying to get out.

"You shush now, little man." Miss Eva's voice was surprisingly strong.

As we went through the gate, Selvin turned to the crowd and said as he raised his hands, "Show's over, folks. Gwan home now. We have private business with Miss Eva."

None of them left, but at least they didn't come right into the yard with us.

"Come on now." Miss Eva invited us onto her porch with a little wave. She reminded me of the birds she made . . . graceful and kind of floaty.

Grandma and Cousin Cecil almost had to drag Olivia up the steps. I knew that I couldn't let my courage fail me now, so I marched up right behind her.

Cousin Cecil introduced us. "Miss Eva, I have before me the two silly girls who came to your porch in the middle of the night."

I stepped forward first. I wanted to get this over with. I have the kind of personality that wants to get the job done as soon as I can. I hate misery.

"Miss Eva, please forgive me for . . ." I stopped. Ugh, here came that glue mouth. I licked my lips and started again. "Miss Eva, I . . . I am Katani Summers and I am very sorry for trespassing on your property." Even Grandma rolled her eyes on that one—I sounded like a criminal.

"I brought you a present . . . something to keep you warm at night." I reached behind my back, climbed the few steps to the veranda, and gave her the brightly wrapped present. "Just so you know, Miss Eva, it's wrapped in really nice yellow paper and I picked a flower from the garden." I paused again, and then I said. "Well, I hope you will forgive me."

The old lady ran her hands all over the gift—feeling every part of it. It was like she was seeing with her hands. Very carefully she unwrapped it, folding the paper without ripping it and holding the flower to her nose. Then she took out the scarf. I could hear murmurs of approval from the crowd.

"Miss Eva, I am the silly girl Katani's grandmother. She has knitted you a lovely pink scarf with a little white bird in the middle."

Miss Eva wrapped the scarf around her neck even though it was about ninety degrees and said in a soft voice, "Pink is pretty, and the birds are my friends. Thank you, Katani."

Olivia was next. I was very proud of my cousin because she took responsibility for everything. Miss Eva chuckled and said that if we had just knocked on the gate, she would have let us in to collect the necklace. I don't know about Olivia, but I felt even more ridiculous.

Miss Eva apologized for not having any drinks to offer us.

"That's okay, Miss Madda . . . Miss Eva," Olivia stammered. "I brought you a gift as well. I made my mother's favorite coconut cake, and we have lemonade and cups and napkins. We can have a little tea party right here."

"Well now, isn't that a lovely thing." Miss Eva seemed genuinely touched.

Olivia and I cut pieces for everyone, even the parade at the gate. The big woman in the purple dress actually said, "I told you they were very nice girls. A very nice family."

Olivia and I could barely choke down our laughter.

As we sat and enjoyed our cake, Miss Eva began to talk. Olivia and I were stunned when she said she couldn't remember how old she was. When Cousin Cecil asked how she came to this part of Jamaica, I thought I saw a tear. She said she came up to get married, but her fiancé left to fight in a war (she couldn't remember which one) and he never came back. She never made enough money to get back to England, where her family came from.

I knew that she must be very lonely because every time we started to leave, she would tell us another story about the birds and old-time Jamaica.

Finally Cousin Cecil said that we wouldn't disturb her anymore but would come back for a visit another day. We all got up to shake her hand. I was surprised to find that her hand, though bony, was not as tough as I thought it would be, since she was constantly carving her birds. I felt very sad that she lived alone with no one to care for her.

Grandma Ruby also shook her hand and complimented her on her bird carvings. She seemed quite pleased about that. When it was Olivia's turn, I heard Miss Eva tell Olivia that she had known it was her all along.

"How do you know this, Miss Eva? You can't see me."

The old lady smiled and grabbed Olivia's arm. "Oh, but I know you, Olivia. I hear your footsteps. They are light and quick and sometimes they dance." Then she added a little shyly, "I hope you come again . . . and please bring your coconut cake with you."

A Night to Remember

That night, before we fell asleep, Olivia and I kept having fits of giggles as one or other of us remembered some silly detail about the crazy "apology parade."

"Did you see that Camille? She must have been combing her hair when she heard. One side of her hair plait and the other side loose."

"Did you see that old man who walked with a cane?" I

asked. "He walked so fast. I think he didn't want to miss any cake."

I listened to Olivia fussing for a while about Miss Eva's fool-fool dog. Somehow, every time she said "fool-fool dog," she sounded funnier and funnier. I started to laugh. She glared at me, then she must have realized how funny she sounded, because she also started to giggle.

"I'm not sorry Miss Eva have him, though. It must be very lonely for her. So it's good she have him. Even though he is soooo annoying." I threw my pillow at her. She was making fun of my Boston slang.

Olivia shook her head. "All those people make a pappy-show of us." She howled at my inquiring expression, then explained, "They made us look like fools."

"Pappy show?" I repeated. I had never heard a stranger word. More laughter. We had to put the pillows over our heads or hold the sheets over our mouths so the grown-ups wouldn't hear us laughing. By the time we fell asleep, we had pretty much laughed away our bad, horrible apology parade, and were ready for whatever tomorrow's adventure would be.

19

Jamaican Holiday

Olivia and I were sitting on the veranda having a game of seriously competitive checkers. I had won two games (yay for me!) and Olivia two. We were smiling and laughing, but underneath, it was war. Checkers war. Personally, I hated to lose. Losing at anything just didn't sit well with me, and it was obvious by the intensity in her eyes that Olivia didn't much enjoy it either. Suddenly Olivia pulled off a huge double jump, and I was forced to crown her queen. Not good news for the Kgirl. Not good at all.

Think, think! I wracked my brain for a move. Olivia wanted to win so badly, she was practically drooling. Of course, at stake was the two dollars we bet. Good thing Grandma Ruby and Cousin Cecil had already left.

"You gwine make a move or what?" Olivia asked impatiently. That girl was *intense*.

"Relax, mon, everything irie. I'm gwine move in a minute," I joked as I doubled-jumped her. Now we were at a standstill. Olivia got up and started pacing. Wow, I hoped we weren't going to get into a serious fight over this. Once, my sister Patrice and I didn't speak for a week when I beat her at a game of checkers.

Suddenly, I saw three steps ahead in the game. Oh, no! There it was . . . the Kgirl was going down. Oooh!

Then we were interrupted by Selvin, who walked in looking all pleased with himself.

"You girls better go pack a bag 'cause I got a number-one day planned. It includes a beach party at a very beautiful resort." Selvin looked all decked out, so I figured this had to be some swanky resort.

"That, Selvin, is music to my ears." I jumped up from the table, but Olivia protested. "Katani, we have to finish the game."

I had one of those moments where I could have just blown her off by saying I wanted to get ready to go. But I stopped myself. I don't like it when people are unfair, so I turned around and pulled out my two dollars and handed them to Olivia.

"Check it out, Olivia, you're going to beat me fair and square, anyway. So here you go."

Olivia took the two dollars. "Yahoo!" she shouted.

"Okay, you don't have to rub it in." I stuck my tongue out at her.

"Yes, I do. It's part of the fun of it." Olivia jumped up, grabbed my arms, and danced me around the kitchen.

Selvin clapped his hands. 'Very nice show! I'm sure Hollywood will be calling tomorrow. But we got to go. Party waiting. Aunt Ruby and Cousin Cecil will meet us at the party."

Olivia and I looked at each other and we both ran for the bedroom. Beach party meant important decisions. Decisions like: how to do your hair, what bathing suit to wear, shorts or a beach dress as a cover-up, a baseball cap or a straw hat, which color nail polish . . . I mean, this stuff is important for a fashion-conscious girl! As far as nail color, I knew immediately which way to go. Gold . . . definitely the gold.

Batting Cricket

When we were in the van, Selvin explained that before we went to the party we could stop and see a cricket game. "Yippee." Olivia waved her arm. "I forgot that my school's team is playing today! Thanks, Selvin!"

"A cricket game?" I exclaimed. "What the heck is that . . . you have bugs chasing each other or something?"

Olivia and Selvin lost it and began hooting with laughter. "You never heard of cricket? Where have you been, girl? It's huge here and in England, too," explained Olivia in between fits of giggles and hiccups.

"Well, I'm American, I've never been to England, and I just got here. Besides, I'm just not that into sports." Really, I didn't think my mistake was *that* funny.

"No, seriously, Katani," Selvin tried to explain. "Cricket is a big game in Jamaica. Everyone follows it. I think you'll like it."

Honestly, I didn't really think I would. I mean, sports were not on the Kgirl list of favorite things. I didn't even follow the Red Sox or the Patriots, and they were huge at home.

"There's the field, Selvin!" Olivia shouted. She was excited to watch the match.

As we walked toward the crowd, I heard someone calling my name. I was shocked. Who in Jamaica knew my name? Usually everybody was calling for Selvin, man-about-Jamaica.

Then I saw him. He was dressed all in white and was waving at us. When we got near the stands, I realized that it was the boy in Olivia's class who had smiled at me when

I was so nervous as the new girl at school. He was in what I figured was his cricket gear—this cool white outfit with these protective pads on his shins—and he had something that looked like a bat in his hand. But the bat wasn't like a baseball bat at all—it was flat. I had to admit, white was definitely working for him.

"I'm glad to see you again," he said with a real nice smile. "I wanted to get your e-mail address and ask if we could write each other. I really liked that speech you gave in class. A girl who's pretty *and* smart."

What?! Who was this guy spilling his guts out to me in the middle of a playing field?! None of the boys at home would *ever* just walk up to a girl and say something like that. Olivia gave me a knowing look. It's not like I had a crush on the guy or anything, but he was really cute. Especially in his white uniform.

"Um, but I don't even know your name," I stuttered, with a shy smile. This boy had me, the cool, confident Kgirl, completely tongue-tied.

"Adrian," he said, flashing me a confident grin. Whoa. This guy definitely had charm and attitude. I fumbled around in my backpack for a pen and paper, and we exchanged addresses. He had a funny screenname: Crickbatjam.

"You want to watch me bat?" he asked. Olivia and I giggled at each other. OF COURSE we wanted to watch him bat!

"Okay," I agreed, and we went to sit with Selvin.

"That Adrian, all the girls like him," she said with a sigh. "You so lucky he say that to you! You must write to me and tell me what he says when he e-mails you." I nodded. I was excited, but I tried to concentrate on the game. It made absolutely no sense at all to me. It looked like a combination of croquet, bowling, and baseball. No one got dirty, and I couldn't figure the scoring at all, but everyone looked cool and spiffy.

Selvin tried to explain the game. "See the two batsmen at either end of the pitch?" I nodded. The pitch, I gathered, was a strip of white ground in the middle of the field. "They're standing before their wickets, the three sticks in the ground. The wicketkeeper squats behind it. Only one faces the bowler. If the ball hits the wicket, or the keeper catches it after he has hit it, he's out. When he hits the ball, he tries to get at least one run by hitting the ball as far away as possible. If a fielder catches the ball, he's also out."

"How does he get the runs?" I asked, because all that happened after the player batted the ball was that one of the fielders picked up the ball and threw it back to the bowler. The batsmen did not move.

"After one of them hits the ball far enough, both batsmen run to the opposite end. The one who bats gets the runs for the number of times they're able to cross to the other end."

"Selvin," I begged, "don't tell me anymore. This would take a hundred years for me to understand."

"Two runs," Olivia said happily, clapping. "If he had batted it to the boundary, he would have got four runs without having to run." The boundary was the edge of the field. "If he bats it over the boundary, he gets six runs, the highest possible score from a hit."

"Mmm-hmm," I said. Olivia was so enthusiastic, I couldn't tell her or Selvin that I was bored out of my mind. I figured cricket must be one of those games that had to grow on you.

Then I heard the crowd shout, "He's out! See, he's been bowled, he's lost his wicket." It was Olivia's friend Marius.

Olivia put her hands over her eyes. "Players hate to lose their wicket." I started to giggle. Olivia gave me a stern look. "It's not funny, Katani."

"Look," she pointed. Adrian was up. Suddenly, the game was a lot more interesting. I wished the boys back home wore cricket outfits. They were so much more stylish then baseball uniforms.

All of sudden the crowd was on their feet. Apparently Adrian had stolen a wicket or something? "He did that for you. You're so gorgeous and all," Olivia teased me.

"Time to go, pickney," Selvin told us. "We must get to the resort."

"I guess I don't get to say good-bye to Adrian," I said a little sadly to Olivia as we left. "Adrian in Jamaica up in a tree, wondering where on earth Katani could be."

"You have his e-mail address," Olivia comforted me. "You e-mail him as soon as you get home, I bet!" She laughed, and I pulled her braid.

"So, Selvin," I asked, when we were back in the van, "what is the name of the resort we are going to?

"The Jamaican Star."

"Selvin!" Olivia screamed. "The Jamaican Star . . . the Jamaican Star." She turned to me. "Oh, my goodness, Katani. This is one of the most beautiful resorts in Jamaica. It's on a beautiful beach, white sand, beautiful pool. If they're having a party, they'll have a band playing reggae music. You gwine love it!"

Oh, boy! I was about to go to heaven in Jamaica.

When we pulled into the lot I saw waiters carrying big trays of tropical fruit down to the beach. My feet began to scrunch up in anticipation of the feel of the sand between my toes.

"Oh, boy! I was about to go to heaven in Jamaica."

Selvin had stashed a couple of trays of Banana Bliss to bring in, so Olivia and I each grabbed one and followed him to the kitchen. There were lots of kids running around and many of them were Olivia's and my age.

As we rounded the corner into the kitchen I saw a group of girls climbing out of a van.

"Olivia—look! It's Leesha and her friends, from Dunn's River Falls."

Surprise Visitors

"Selvin—my girls are here. Can Katani and I go party with them?" Olivia pleaded.

"Sure, but help me first. We need to bring these trays in."

I looked over at Olivia and by the look on her face I guessed that she didn't want our new friends seeing her carry trays in. But before I could say anything, Leesha's group was running across the parking lot to meet us.

Olivia had her proud look on, and I was afraid that she would ignore Leesha, just to save face. But then Leesha was at our side and gushing over Nana's Banana Bliss.

"Olivia, is this your family business?! I love Banana Bliss. Whenever we're in Jamaica my mother buys it on Friday mornings so we have it for the weekend. I could eat it every day. It's so yummy."

Olivia's faced turned pink with pleasure and she looked at Selvin. "Can we give them one piece?"

Selvin nodded and pulled a big, fat piece off the tray. The girls squealed with delight. "Tell these pretty friends of yours that you will meet them at the beach after we drop the trays off," Selvin instructed us.

"Olivia," Leesha said between bites, "you guys should meet us at the bandstand. There is a rumor that Sean Kingston might drop by. He's in Jamaica right now." They ran off dancing and jamming to a Sean Kingston beat.

"Sean Kingston," I screamed. He was the hottest hip-hop artist around. I couldn't believe my luck.

Seeing my over-the-top excitement, Selvin decided to put a damper on things by teasing, "You know, everytime there is a beach party, someone say, 'Sean is coming,' and the 'beautiful girls' dance around like chickens. And what you think, mon? Mr. Sean Kingston nowhere to be found."

"A girl can always dream," I said, head in the air, and I walked ahead of him with my tray. *Sean Kingston, Sean Kingston, please, please let him be here*, I prayed. Seeing Sean Kingston would be like somebody flew into space and brought me down a piece of the moon. I practically danced all the way to the kitchen.

As soon as Olivia and I found a place to put our trays in the kitchen, we were out of there. Neither of us wanted to miss one more minute of the beach party.

"Aunt Ruby and Dad are probably already here," Olivia said. "Let's go!"

Beach Party

When we got down to the beach there was such a crowd that I couldn't see my grandma or Cousin Cecil but I did see the coolest swimming pool ever, right on the beach. It was designed like a pirate ship . . . partygoers were shooting down the waterslides, floating down Blackbeard's lazy river in what looked like painted rubber tires, and swimming under little bridges, and walking the plank. It looked like fun to the max!

"Look, Katani. Leesha's got a chair for us."

I could see Leesha waving to us from the deep end of the pool. Kayla was about to jump off the plank, and Olivia and I raced to stake out beach lounge chairs next to where the girls had dropped their stuff.

"Let's jump in, Katani. They are already setting up the stage for the band and I don't want to miss the dancing. It's my favorite." Olivia flipped off her shorts and the funky red shirt that she had tied at her waist and just dived right into the pool. She swam her way through a bunch of kids up to Leesha, Megan, and Kayla.

I, on the other hand, was thinking, *My hair is going to look really awful if I get it wet.* I watched a young girl walk by whose hair had dried all natural and curly. Mmm! Then it came to me—a vision. I was in Jamaica, and I was going to have fun and do it up Jamaica-style. I tossed my beach bag onto the lounge chair, shimmied out of my beach dress, slipped the earrings out of my ears, put my flip-flops under my chair, and jumped onto a green tube with a little palm tree attached to it.

I floated by Leesha and Olivia and in my most horrible crow voice I began to sing along with the reggae band that had just begun to play.

Leesha, her friends, and Olivia were laughing so hard, they couldn't stop. I mean, I knew I was being funny, but even I knew I wasn't that funny. Finally Olivia pointed, and I turned my head to look. I didn't really register for a minute until I heard his voice.

"Hello, Katani. I'm thinking that maybe you are still pretty and smart, but I am sorry to tell you"—he paused for one awful second—"you cannot sing, girl, at all."

Disaster city! The one boy in Jamaica who thought I was cool had now seen me make a complete fool of myself. There was nowhere to run. Nowhere to hide. I had to make one of those decisions that all kids hate. Do I get mean and evil and pout because everyone saw me be silly and stupid? Or . . . do I go with the flow? I decided to go with the flow.

"Maybe you would like this song better?" I smiled sweetly at Adrian and joined in again with the band. *"Yellow bird up high in a banana tree . . . ,"* I sang loudly and proudly.

The next thing I knew, I was underwater. Adrian had dived into the pool and helped Olivia, Leesha, Megan, and Kayla spin me around and flip me upside down. *Kgirl, you have been dumped!* I thought as I came up sputtering and laughing and spewing water from my nostrils.

When I wiped the water out of my eyes I looked across to the dance floor. There, who should I see in front of me but

Precious and Mr. Biggs, dancing with a group of other couples! And out of the corner of my eye I saw Nana's Banana Bliss reality TV show unfolding before my eyes. I grabbed Olivia's hand for support. "Look!" I hissed at her. She stopped splashing around and turned too.

Grandma Ruby and Cousin Cecil were walking by the dance floor when they both saw Mr. Biggs and Precious. Oh, Grandma Ruby was looking mad . . . really mad, and Selvin was running toward them, yelling, "Ruby, Ruby, you are right. We have been betrayed."

I never climbed out of a pool so fast in my life. Something was wrong here. Very wrong. Olivia was hot on my trail, and our friends were following her. This was my worst nightmare. I didn't know what was worse: a showdown in front of people I did know or didn't know.

By the time I got to Grandma, she was accusing Precious of betraying her. Precious was crying, and Mr. Biggs—that huge, scary man—was looking like he had absolutely no idea what to do. Selvin and Cousin Cecil were staring at him, and Precious was trying to explain. Worse, a crowd had gathered. We were going from Beach Party to Beach Party Disaster.

"But Miss Ruby, Precious is an honest woman who loves her job . . . a professional woman," a nervous Mr. Biggs tried to explain.

"Who wants to put *us* out of business spying for *you*," Grandma Ruby retorted.

"No, no!" Precious pleaded. "Please, Miss Ruby, I am here with Mr. Biggs, but it is not what you think. What proof do you have that I have done this to Banana Bliss?"

Grandma was silent for a moment.

"We saw you!" I suddenly exclaimed. Everyone looked at me. I looked over at Olivia, gulped, and went on. "That night at the bakery. Olivia and I saw you get into Mr. Biggs's SUV and drive away. And before that, I saw you talking to him in his SUV outside the bakery."

"Katani?" Grandma seemed surprised. "Did you know what Precious was up to and didn't tell Cousin Cecil and me?"

"But, Grandma, I thought you knew," I said. Now I was really confused. "When Olivia and I were explaining what happened, Cousin Cecil said he already knew all about why Precious was at the bakery that night."

"The cell phone—she said she forgot her cell phone, and went back to get it at the bakery. That is what I knew," a confused Cousin Cecil answered.

Finally Precious collected herself. "I did go to the bakery that night to get my cell phone. But what these girls saw is right—it was Mr. Biggs that drove me there. I was going to tell you Miss Ruby, Mr. Cousin Cecil, but Denzel—er, Mr. Biggs . . . and I—we have only been seeing each other for a couple of weeks." There was a little gasp from the crowd. Precious was *dating* Mr. Biggs?! "I didn't want to make that public yet," she went on. "I love my job and I am very loyal to Miss Faith and Banana Bliss. Besides"—she looked over at the embarrassed big man—"him a big flirt and I don't know if I will stay with him or not." Precious put her nose in the air as the crowd clapped and whistled.

Now it all made sense, why Precious was hanging around Mr. Biggs so much. They were dating! But that didn't make her a spy. I felt really bad for accusing her, and I suspected Grandma Ruby did too.

"This is a pretty bad scene," Olivia whispered in my ear. No kidding. The Banana Bliss drama was beyond embarrassing. It was super humiliating! I looked over at Adrian. What was he thinking about the pretty, smart girl and her family now?

"Precious, I think we all owe you an apology," Grandma Ruby said sincerely. "It wasn't fair for us to jump to conclusions like that. I am very sorry, and I'm sure these girls are too." She looked at Olivia and me with a look that said, *Your turn*.

"I'm sorry, Precious," we said at the same time.

Cousin Cecil stuck out his hand. "I knew in my heart you would never betray Banana Bliss, Precious," he said. She took his hand, and they shook firmly.

Grandma Ruby shook her head. "What do we do now, with all of this silliness?" Then she wagged her finger at Mr. Biggs. "You have started all of this with your competitive ways. You have more trucks and more people. Why don't you just leave Faith alone to make our Bliss?" Then she said the fighting words: "Our banana bread is better than yours, anyway."

20

Banana Bread Showdown

"Oh!" Mr. Biggs said. "So that's how it's gonna be. If you think your bread is so good, then we should have a competition here and now."

"Competition? Competition?" exclaimed Grandma. "There's no competition. Your banana bread can't compete with our Banana Bliss."

The hotel manager, who had just arrived to see what all the fuss was about, looked slightly alarmed. Selvin, who knew the manager very well, hastily introduced him. "This is Ruby Fields, Aunt Faith's niece. She's come from the States to help out at the bakery while Aunt Faith's in the hospital." He turned to my grandma. "This is Mr. MacFarlane, Ruby. He looks after purchases." Mr. MacFarlane nodded, but he was still looking a little frightened.

"What happen, Biggs?" Selvin asked. "Giving away more free samples? You trying to steal this customer too?"

"Aren't you ashamed of yourself?" Grandma accosted him. "Trying to take away an old lady's living?"

I held my breath, but Mr. Biggs just laughed. "It's a free country," he said. "All's fair in love, war, and commerce."

"Hmph!" Grandma snorted. "So be it. We can't fight your free giveaways, but we can settle whose bread is better . . . right now. Go get the bread."

"Mine is better," he grumbled.

I shook my head from side to side. What was my grandma doing? A banana bread competition here and now? I looked yearningly at the ocean. That's where I should be right now.

"Selvin. Get Faith on the phone," Grandma Ruby commanded. "I won't do this unless she agrees. It's her business."

Selvin ran back to the van to get his cell phone.

Banana Versus Banana

I thought Grandma Ruby would be nervous. But when I looked over at her, I knew I was wrong. The principal of Abigail Adams Junior High was steely-eyed—like when she had to break up a fight on the playground. Nobody was going to mess with my grandma, not even Mr. Biggs of the Manteca Bay Bakery Company.

Trays of banana bread were being brought out to the tables lining the pool. The place looked like a banana bread convention! Selvin came running back with his cell phone and gave Ruby a thumbs-up. "Faith say, 'Believe in Nana's Banana Bliss.'"

Grandma Ruby smiled calmly and turned to the man in the cowboy hat. "Let the competition begin, Mr. Biggs."

The waiters passed around Banana Bread and Banana Bliss to the people gathered outside by the pool. There must have been more than fifty of them! It was agonizing watching people chew and chew and chew. *Enough already . . . one bite should tell them*, I thought as I chewed on my nails. "Katani, you going to ruin your nail polish," Olivia scolded me. I stopped immediately. Got to protect the look, after all.

Finally, the manager asked for a show of hands . . . and . . . it was over almost as soon as it began.

Nana's Banana Bliss had won almost unanimously!

"Yeah!" I yelled. Olivia, Selvin, and I jumped around like a bunch of crazy roosters. Cousin Cecil was smiling like I had never seen him smile before, and Grandma, she sat down in a chair and stared out at the ocean with a little smile. Then I saw Cousin Cecil and Selvin chatting with a pretty little woman who turned out to be Chloe from Devon House. Hmm. Nice. *Cousin Cecil and Chloe, sitting in a tree* . . . I would have to tell Olivia.

I had to give it to Mr. Biggs. He was a professional through and through. He shook Grandma's hand, sat down next to her, and they began to chat. I heard the words "Banana . . . share . . . big island . . . small business." Sounded good to me.

Suddenly, Adrian and Olivia's friend Marius came madly running toward us. They were shouting and waving their hands, yelling something.

"Him come, Sean Kingston come."

Olivia and I raced down the beach with the growing crowd. One of the biggest hip-hop artists in the world was here at *our* beach party! We passed Leesha, Megan, and Kayla as we ran, and they fell in beside us, laughing and shouting. Everyone was running so fast that if someone had seen us from the air, they would think we were being chased by invaders from another planet.

Then all of us heard them—the words "Beautiful girls . . ." floating back to us. Sean Kingston was singing my favorite song! Adrian grabbed my hand, and we danced our way down to the beach.

To: Maeve, Isabel, Avery, Charlotte
From: Katani
Subject: Crazy trip!

Hey, BSG! Grandma and I are headed back
to the airport this afternoon. This
vacation seemed like it was only about
thirty seconds long! I can't WAIT to see
my BSG and show you all the incredible
pics I took, but I'm soooo sad to leave
Jamaica too. Magic memories for days—
dancing with dolphins, climbing up a
waterfall, jerk chicken, man-eating
goats, and, oh yeah, a Sean Kingston
concert on the beach! Hell-oooo! How
much luck can Kgirl have? Specific and
very cool details to follow.

We definitely have to make this a
vacation destination for the BSG one
day. You all would like it here so
much—it's like there's something for
everyone! Like, Isabel, the colors here
are AMAZING! Blue water, green palm
leaves, big juicy fruits in all kinds of
wacky shades . . . you get the picture.
Charlotte, there's so much cool history
here you could read about. Avery—there's
tons of outdoorsy stuff to do! Even the
most uncoordinated girl on this island
(that's me!) got her exercise on. And
three words for you, Maeve: ISLAND BEACH

PARTY. Do I have to say anything else,
girl?

But if we do make a BSG trip to
Jamaica, you girls will definitely want
someone to explain all the crazy stuff
people say and do and eat here! Maybe
my cousin Selvin will take us around.
He's the best! I had to learn it all
pretty fast, but I think now I can
spill some total insider info about
visiting Jamaica. Like, if you ever
see a goat, run in the other direction
as fast as you can! (Trust me—I know
from personal experience. VERY personal
experience! Picture me, the Kgirl, with
a goat munching on her fave polka-dotted
pj's . . . not pretty.)

And it's not all beaches and tropical
drinks in Jamaica. I mean, there are
some really beautiful beaches and really
really tasty fruit juices (like coconut
water—right from the coconut!), but
there's also these cool mountains and
towns and farms, just like anywhere.
I didn't even know that my own family
lived on a farm until we got here! It's
nothing like High Hopes Riding Stable,
but it's very pretty. I thought Jamaica
was going to be one long runway walk on
the beach, but chilling with my fam and

finding out how people really live here turned out to be way more interesting. Char—I might just have to sign up for your kids travel club with Nick and Chelsea.

Actually, the strangest thing I found here was something . . . someone . . . I brought with me—Grandma Ruby! Now you're thinking, "Kgirl has completely lost her mind on that island!" right? But I'm totally for real. It's like I got to see this whole other side of my grandma. You know how she is usually absolutely in control, on top of everything. She always knows what to do. But in Jamaica, she was the opposite! She actually messed up on a couple of things, and she even ended up with a bag of flour on her head one day! (Can you even IMAGINE that?! AAJH Principal Ruby Fields completely covered in fluffy white flour— total LOL moment.)

But I messed up on some things too. I got in so much trouble with my cousin Olivia! You would love Olivia—she's 100 percent BSG material. But we made a HUGE mistake, got completely busted, and had to apologize in front of the whole village! I'll tell you the whole, sad story when I get home.

So basically the Kgirl business-and-life lesson for this vacation is that things aren't always what they seem. You never know when a scary old witch could turn out to be a really nice, friendly old woman, so you can't judge a book by its cover. Or . . . you can't judge an island by its beaches! Well, maybe you can. Jamaican beaches rock!

And if you want the REAL insider 411, here's a Kgirl list of what to do (and what NOT to do) in Jamaica:

1. Try the banana bread with guava jelly. Soooo tasty. But make sure it's Nana's Banana Bliss!

2. Take a horseback ride in the ocean. (And say hello to Lazarus, the best horse in Jamaica!)

3. Drink coconut water straight from the coconut.

4. Climb the waterfall at Dunn's River Falls. If Kgirl can do it, anybody can!

5. Make sure you have a giant bottle of icy cold water nearby when you eat jerk chicken. (Trust me!)

6. Never steal a comb from a River Mumma!

7. Go for the guava ice cream at Devon House. Mmmm.

8. Don't even try to distract a mean old dog with a piece of meat—it won't work!

9. Dance with dolphins.

10. Don't wear a miniskirt to church, no matter how cute it is. I recommend a long, flowy, island-y skirt instead.

And, most of all . . . STAY AWAY FROM THE GOATS!

TTYL,
Kgirl

Katani's Jamaican Holiday

BOOK EXTRAS

1. What color is the cover of Katani's Island Inspiration notebook?
   A. red, white, and blue
   B. turquoise, lavender, and Tuscan gold
   C. yellow, black, and green
   D. pink, purple, and baby blue

2. How does Spotty the goat react when Katani meets him for the first time?
   A. He lets her pet him.
   B. He chases her out of the pen.
   C. He hides behind Olivia.
   D. He licks her hand.

3. In Cousin Cecil's story, what does Orrin take from the River Mumma?
   A. a comb
   B. a cup
   C. a mirror
   D. a book

4. What kind of pet does Ol' Madda Bird have?
   A. a bird
   B. a dog
   C. a cat
   D. a monkey

5. Where does Olivia find her missing necklace?
   A. under her pillow
   B. in her desk at school
   C. up in a tree
   D. on Ol' Madda Bird's veranda

6. Who runs into Olivia and Katani outside the bakery at midnight?
A. Precious
B. Cousin Cecil
C. Miss Gloria
D. Leesha

7. What kind of ice cream does Katani have at Devon House?
A. mango
B. papaya
C. guava
D. pineapple

8. Who gives Katani a beautiful beaded bracelet?
A. Chloe
B. Selvin
C. Olivia
D. Grandma Ruby

9. What does Katani make as a gift for Ol' Madda Bird?
A. a blanket
B. a pair of socks
C. a hat
D. a scarf

10. What sport is Adrian playing when Katani meets him?
A. baseball
B. cricket
C. soccer
D. basketball

Katani's Patois Dictionary

Patois Words

banyan tree: a large spreading tree. It spreads by sending down aerial roots that kids love to swing on.

bobo dread: dressed in long robes and tight turbans, the bobo dreads are a sect within the Rastafarian community. They live apart in their own areas and make straw mats and brooms for sale.

bumptious: presumptuous or pushy

dem: them

dey: they

escoveitch: literally "pickled." Escoveitch fish is fried, then steeped in a mixture of hot vinegar, pepper, onions, and pimento seeds.

fass: inquisitive

favor: resemble

fi: for

fool-fool: very foolish. In Jamaican patois, doubling a word increases its intensity.

gwan: go on

gwine: going to

irie: okay

Jah-Jah: the name Rastafarians use for god

mash: smash

mek: make

mon: man

pappy show: puppet show

peenie-wallies: fireflies

pickney: child

pickney dem: children

plait: braid; braided

Rastafarian: also called just "Rasta." Rasta, or the Rastafari movement, is a religious movement started in Jamaica.

tups: a little

Patois Phrases

So the barrel come: So you got something new. Many Jamaicans who live abroad regularly send home barrels of food and clothing for their families.

Me deh rock so: I am rocking like this.

Come mek we dance and sing: Let us dance and sing.

Mind dem own business: Pay attention to their own problems.

They come long time?: Have they been here long?

We just reach: We just got here.

What gone bad a mawning, cyan come good a evening: Something bad in the morning won't be good in the evening.

Empty barrel mek the most noise: Empty barrels make the

most noise. (People who know the least about something often talk the most about it.)

By and by, yuh wi si: By and by, you will see. (You'll find out eventually.)

To make a pappy show of someone: to make someone look foolish

Ah fi mi pickney dese: These are my children

Mi mek dem in mi image: I made them in my image

Mi love dem and look out fi dem: I love them, I take care of them

Jammin' Jamaican Facts

Map It!

Jamaica is the third-largest island in the Caribbean and the largest English-speaking island. It spans 4,244 square miles and sits entirely surrounded by the Caribbean Sea, ninety miles southwest of Cuba.

What's in a Name?

The name *Jamaica* comes from the Arawak word *Xaymaca*, meaning "land of wood and water." Words like *barbecue, canoe, hurricane*, and *tobacco* come from the language of the first colonists of Jamaica, the Arawak-speaking group of people now known as the Tainos.

Land Ho!

In the seventeenth century, Port Royal in Jamaica was the base for many notorious buccaneers and pirates. Among these were Blackbeard, Calico Jack, Anne Bonny, and Henry Morgan. Port Royal was known as the richest and wickedest city on earth until it was destroyed by a violent earthquake in 1692. Three quarters of the town sank that day!

Out of Many, One People

Jamaica's motto, "Out of Many, One People," reflects a rich and diverse culture. Jamaica is populated by more than two and a half million people. African and English influences dominate the culture, but the Spanish, Irish, Indians, Chinese, and Germans have all left their mark in food, speech, music, and dance. Jamaicans can tour the world without leaving their island!

Spouting Off

Ocho Rios means "eight rivers" in Spanish, but there aren't eight rivers near the town. Actually, the name is a corruption of the Spanish word *chorreras*, meaning "spouts" or "waterfalls." But most Jamaicans just call it Ochi.

Tee Time

Jamaica can lay claim to the oldest golf course in the western hemisphere. Following the introduction of golf in Scotland, a nine-hole course was built in Mandeville, Jamaica, at the first country club in the New World. The Duke of Manchester opened Mandeville Golf Club in 1865—*before* many of Europe's most famous courses were built.

Make It a Clean Sweep

In Jamaica, it's an old custom to place a broom upside down behind a door in your house when you want an unwanted guest to go away.

Pipe Down!

Falmouth, Jamaica, had piped water before New York City! Way back in 1799, a twenty-foot waterwheel was installed on land near the Martha Brae River. This giant wheel was turned by the current of the stream and emptied about one hundred gallons of water per revolution into a wooden trough. Then the water flowed through a six-inch pipe into a large tank in the town square of Falmouth. Even today, people call this part of town Water Square.

Spice It Up

The spice that gives Jamaican jerk its special kick is called pimento. Pimento is the only spice indigenous to Jamaica, which makes Jamaican jerk a very special cuisine!

Nana's Banana Bliss Recipe

Ingredients
2 eggs, beaten well
½ cup (one stick) butter, at room temperature
4 very ripe bananas, peeled
1 ½ cups flour
1 cup sugar
¼ teaspoon salt
1 teaspoon baking soda
Nana's secret ingredient: ¼ cup shredded coconut

Directions
1. Preheat oven to 350°.
2. Cut butter into small pieces and mix into the beaten eggs with a pastry blender.
3. In a separate bowl, mash bananas.
4. Combine bananas with egg mixture.
5. Mix dry ingredients together, including Nana's secret ingredient.
6. Add dry ingredients to banana mixture.
7. Pour batter into lightly greased 9" x 5" x 3" loaf pan.
8. Bake on middle rack of oven for 50 minutes. Test with knife—if it doesn't come out clean, bake another 10 minutes.
9. Allow to cool for 15 minutes, then invert onto rack and let sit until completely cooled.
10. Optional Glaze (for fancy parties): Mix 1 cup confectioner's sugar, enough water for spreading consistency, and 1 tsp. vanilla. Spread on top of bread.

Share the Next

BEACON STREET GIRLS

Special Adventure

Isabel's Texas Two-Step

Isabel's sister Elena Maria is turning fifteen, and the Martinez family is celebrating her quinceañera at Uncle Hector's cattle ranch in San Antonio! Isabel thinks everything about San Antonio is awesome (except for her annoying cousin Ricardo). The Southwestern art gives her all sorts of ideas for new drawings.

But Elena has turned into Quincezilla—you'd think no one has ever turned fifteen before—and Isabel feels like she's invisible. It's a good thing there's so much to see and do in San Antonio. And when Isabel and her cousin get stranded in a cave during a thunder and lightning storm, they make an amazing discovery!

Check out the Beacon Street Girls at

www.beaconstreetgirls.com

Aladdin M!X

Collect all the BSG books today!

#1 Worst Enemies/Best Friends
Yikes! As if being the new girl isn't bad enough ... Charlotte just made the biggest cafeteria blunder in the history of Abigail Adams Junior High.

☐ **READ IT!**

#2 Bad News/Good News
Charlotte can't believe it. Her father wants to move away again, and the timing couldn't be worse for the Beacon Street Girls.

☐ **READ IT!**

#3 Letters from the Heart
Life seems perfect for Maeve and Avery ... until they find out that in seventh grade, the world can turn upside down just like that.

☐ **READ IT!**

#4 Out of Bounds
Can the Beacon Street Girls bring the house down at Abigail Adams Junior High's Talent Show? Or will the Queens of Mean steal the show?

☐ **READ IT!**

#5 Promises, Promises
Elections for class president are underway, and the Beacon treet Girls are right in the middle of it all. The drama escalates when election posters start to disappear.

☐ **READ IT!**

#6 Lake Rescue
Big time fun awaits the Beacon Street Girls and the rest of the seventh grade. The class is heading to Lake Rescue in New Hampshire for outdoor adventure.

☐ **READ IT!**

#7 Freaked Out
The party of the year is just around the corner. What happens when the party invitations are given out ... but not to everyone?

☐ **READ IT!**

#8 Lucky Charm
Marty is missing! The BSG begin a desperate search for their beloved doggie mascot which leads them to an unexpected and famous person.

☐ **READ IT!**

#9 Fashion Frenzy

Also . . . Our Special Adventure Series:

Free Sean Kingston Song Download!

The first 1,000 girls to log on to

www.beaconstreetgirls.com

can download Sean Kingston's hit song,
"Beautiful Girls" for FREE.

BEACON STREET GIRLS®

Enter to win a trip to

JAMAICA

for you and your family at

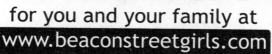

www.beaconstreetgirls.com

For more information on family vacations, please visit

www.visitjamaica.com/family